I0741747

THE AGENCY
Beyond the Call of Duty

By

Cherif Sidiali

www.hexagonblue.com

The Agency
Beyond the Call of Duty

1st Edition Published in 2014 by Hexagon Blue

ISBN13 978-0-9729958-3-2

www.hexagonblue.com

Table of Contents

Chapter 1
ON THE MOVE

The months of February and March were the busiest time of the year for George Munssif. As the head of an international supply company, he travelled the world negotiating business deals and closing sales. On a breezy and cold early Sunday morning on February 5th, George was waiting for his ride to the airport. With his neatly packed Calvin Klein leather travel bag set by the front door of his recently bought town house, he waited, looking out his living room window for the cab to pull up. George had done this sort of work for some years and very much enjoyed travelling to unknown places. His place was spacious and comfortable, the furniture was neatly arranged, and the floors were all covered with expensive Persian rugs he brought back with him from his trips to different countries. The light colored furniture with an accent of dark wall paint made George's house modern and stylish.

There was nothing particular about George Munssif that would make him unusual. However, one thing did stand out about him: his background. George's parents were Christian Lebanese. His father, Albert Munssif, was an architect by trade, and his mother, Isabella Khudry, worked part time as a nurse. They came to the U.S. in late 70s. The decision to uproot his family wasn't easy, but circumstances beyond Albert's control forced him to move. In Washington, DC for the first time, he knew nobody and had a difficult time adjusting to the lifestyle.

The Munssifs lived in DC for 2 years before Albert was able to transfer to Cleveland, Ohio, wanting to take his family to a less crowded place that didn't attract much attention. Cleveland, known for the internationally-renowned Cleveland Orchestra, the Cleveland Museum of Art and the Fine Arts Garden, the Cleveland Opera, and the Cleveland Shakespeare Festival, sounded like the ideal place for Albert and his family to settle. He was very much a patron of the opera and symphony.

Albert was immediately placed in a small commercial architectural firm making decent money, and after few weeks searching for a job, Isabella joined a private medical clinic. In Lebanon she had been a medical doctor, but could not work as a doctor in the States, as her educational credentials and her experience were not up to the U.S. medical standards. Life wasn't that bad after all. Years of experience in the medical field made her work easy, and she already spoke English, which made it even easier for her to adjust.

Sometimes the stress was little too much for George's parents, and at times they even regretted leaving Lebanon, where they worked less and enjoyed life more, but Albert was willing to put up with all the inconveniences for the sake of George's future. Despite being raised in a western society, George's parents insisted on raising him with mostly Arab and Lebanese values. They spoke only Arabic at home although they were all fluent in French and English. In Cleveland they made new friends, some of whom were Arabs, to help them overcome missing their home.

As time went by, George grew to be an accomplished young man. At the age of 16, after ten years spent in Cleveland, he became one of the top pianists in Ohio, and was even invited to perform with the Cleveland Orchestra. George liked all the attention and enjoyed playing the piano; he was so good at it that he decided to major in music at college and make it his career. That made his parents so proud, especially his dad, who thought that moving George to the U.S. was paying off.

The same week George turned 16, Isabella landed a better-paying job as the head nurse for the department of gynecology with University Hospitals at the McDonald Women's Hospital. Being in the spot light as a known pianist with a bright future and a 4.0 student in Eleanor Gerson High School in Ohio gave George a unique chance to mingle with high profile personalities such as the Governor, the Mayor, the Attorney General, and many other influential people in the state. George was on top of the world; nothing could stop him or even slow him down from going to college and becoming the great pianist he dreamed of becoming one day. A music scholarship had already been secured at one of the top music schools in North America, the Eastman School in Rochester, New York - an exclusive school of music that admitted only about 13% of applicants.

Life was great, and the Munssifs were quite satisfied with how things were going, until one sad summer day on June 12th, 1988 when Albert was diagnosed with a rare form of cardiovascular disease known as *cardiac hydatid cysts with intracavitary expansion*. This was a surprise to many who knew Albert through the years, as he never complained of any illness. He always took care of his health, didn't smoke, didn't drink, and had no apparent signs of any sickness. The tests and exams conducted did not reveal any abnormalities, and even some of the best doctors in the field couldn't tell Isabella exactly what the real problem was with Albert's case. Tests of all sorts were conducted in some top hospitals in the country. Some doctors thought maybe it was a tumor that had manifested itself with no previous warnings; others believed it could be a mild case of cardiomegaly, but there was no definite prognosis.

This news hit the Munssif family hard, particularly George, as he was enthusiastic about the prospects of moving to

Rochester, New York. At this point hopes for Albert's health were fading, forcing him to reduce his work schedule to part time and spending more time between doctors and hospitals. George did everything he could to accept the situation and deal with it as best as he could. On March 19th, 1989 Albert passed away in his sleep at home at age 55. The shock for Isabella was devastating and traumatized her will to do anything for a long time. She took a leave of absence from work and stayed home.

Albert's wish was to be buried in Lebanon. He wanted to be interred next to his parents in a small cemetery about 10 kilometers outside Beirut. Isabella respected that wish and made arrangements for his body to be transported to Beirut. For a short while she played with the idea of moving back to Lebanon, but what would happen to George? Uprooting him again didn't sound like a good idea; moving by herself wasn't ideal either, now that she felt integrated into American life. And beside all that, what would she do in Lebanon? Life had changed so much that it would be difficult for her to find employment.

George and Isabella made the trip with Albert for the last time. They fulfilled his wish and stayed a few days before returning to Cleveland. Upon their landing in Cleveland-Hopkins International Airport, Isabella exploded in tears. George stood there watching his mom silently; he knew the reason but was strong enough to hold back his emotions. They retrieved their luggage and took a cab home.

The house felt like an ice block without Albert, cold and meaningless. Isabella set her handbag on the dining room table, removed her light blue jacket, and threw it on the couch. She sat down on Albert's favorite chair, a gift for his 54th birthday. She had joked with him that he was old and he needed a comfortable chair. She ran her hand gently over the armchair trying to stop the tears streaming down her long, thin face. That day went by slowly and seemed like an eternity for both of them.

Later that evening, Isabella decided to check the phone messages. A few phone calls from Albert's friends wanting to stop by to visit, a couple more calls from her work, and one important call was for George from the Cleveland Opera requesting him to play for an upcoming state event. However, George was in no mood to even think about that now. His mom gave him the message, but he didn't show any interest or even a sign of excitement. That same evening, Isabella decided to sort out Albert's effects. George had always liked the collection of tiny key chains his dad had amassed. Albert had collected well over 700 key chains from all over the world. As a child, George had a habit of sneaking into his dad's office to admire the collection.

A few days after their return from Lebanon, it was time to start thinking about the future. Isabella decided to go back to work and George finally opened up the piano sat down, pulled the bench closer and lightly stroked the piano keys. He started playing Beethoven's famous composition *"Fur Elise,"* which he had mastered long ago. But halfway into playing it, he changed his mind, stopped, and wrapped his arms around his head with his elbows pressed tightly against his ears. He stayed in that position for few minutes before returning to playing again, this time composing something of his own in memory of Albert. He pulled out his music notes, set them up, and started moving his fingertips between the piano keys with grace and confidence. He called his piece "The Day We Met".

George spent countless hours and days perfecting his new composition. He wanted Albert to be proud of him again, and after two weeks he finally was happy with his work and played it for his mom. Isabella knew her son very well. She knew all he was keeping inside since Albert's death would eventually come out in his passionate playing. She hugged him, wiping her eyes and smiling as if Albert could see them both.

The healing started settling into the Munssifs' house as weeks and months passed. Isabella and George began to look forward, and time moved quickly. When George was a few weeks shy of turning 17 years, he made plans to move to Rochester, New York. He convinced Isabella to start looking for a medical job in New York, as there was no way he would leave her behind in Cleveland. Spring being the hottest time of the year for the real estate business, Isabella and George made preparations to put the house up for sale.

They made contact with an agent to whom they were referred by one of Isabella's acquaintances and agreed to meet at the house. They hired Kathy Wetfield. Her name fit her. She was in her late 50s, short, and spoke with a New York accent. Kathy had been in real estate forever and knew all there was to know about bank loans, financing, contractors, and building codes. She learned all this from working with two well-known Jewish brothers who owned some brokerage firms and construction companies in New York. After few years working for the two brothers, Kathy decided to take the plunge and open her own office, but the brokerage business being a cut throat business, she didn't last very long on her own. She lost big and was forced to file for bankruptcy to save whatever she had left. That unforgettable experience and her health issues caused by the financial ruin influenced her move from New York to Cleveland in the late 70s. She wanted to start fresh somewhere else.

Isabella liked Kathy's knowledge of real estate and was impressed by her credentials; George, however, didn't care much for her. Maybe because he wasn't ready to give up the times he spent in that house and saw Kathy invading his very own memories. The discussion went on for couple of hours hammering out all the details before they signed the contract with Kathy. Two and a half weeks later, an offer came in, and Isabella wanted the deal to close fast so they could move, but George again was having trouble letting go. After much discussion, they accepted the offer and had three weeks to move out.

That was enough time to get to New York. Having never been to New York before, they did not know what to expect once there. Isabella still didn't have any idea about the job situation; the only sure thing was George's music school. They made it to Rochester, where Kathy arranged for a temporary place to rent until they figured out what to do. The rental, although in an upscale area, was small and barely accommodated some of the fine furniture Isabella had collected over time. The rest was put into storage.

They settled in Maplewood, a northwest neighborhood south of Eastman Business Park, between the Genesee River and Dewey Avenue. The area was pleasant, with its green space stretching along the river, parkways, and the Maplewood Rose Garden. George's school was a short distance from the new place, which gave Isabella peace of mind amidst all the horrible stories she heard—even from Kathy—about living in New York.

The following fall, George started his program and was mostly satisfied with how things were going. Isabella was looking for work and was quite sure she'd find something, given her impressive credentials and recommendation letters written by some of highly recognized and admired doctors in the nation.

The Eastman Music Conservatory within the Rochester University was like nothing George had ever seen. He was even more excited about the Sibley Music Library, named after Hiram Watson Sibley. The library took up three floors, with 45,000 square feet of space. Its collections included items from 11th Century manuscripts to recent compositions and recordings. The library was most famous for housing the original drafts of

Debussy's impressionistic masterpiece *"La Mer"*, along with the largest musical collection in North America. The first time George came face-to-face with this marvelous place, he stood there like a kid in a candy store before proceeding to move from one aisle to the next, fascinated by the thousands of items at his disposal at any day and time. While George was enjoying this extraordinary newly fulfilled desire, Isabella wasn't so lucky with her job prospects. However, she wasn't concerned at all with her situation, as long as George was happy and living his dream.

Later in the semester, George developed a special friendship with Mr. Howard Miller, his instructor, who saw in George something unique. Everybody at Eastman knew who Mr. Howard Miller was, a middle-aged, cranky professor, who didn't give consideration to anyone's feelings. Despite this, for some strange reason he had lasted for years at Eastman, maybe because he was the most senior faculty, or maybe there was nobody who knew about music as much as he did. Students, other faculty, and even management put up with his attitude.

Howard Miller had had some ups and downs in his life. He lived alone after getting divorced from his wife. He left the house to his ex-wife, packed the few things he had, and moved out to a small, rented flat on the other side of town. The two bedroom apartment was roomy, had floor-to-ceiling windows all around, and on a clear day the sun made its way in to every corner. His olive green couch and two dark red recliners filled his living room. One of his rooms was dedicated to his music library and political readings. He was into politics as much as music, and filled the room with every imaginable codex imaginable. The other he used as a bedroom where he rarely slept, sleeping most of the time on one of the recliners or the couch.

Looking at him, it was obvious that the sufferings and overpowering circumstances from his failed marriage, to his son's death in a tragic car accident, and not seeing eye-to-eye with his oldest daughter since the divorce, caused the somber mood he was constantly fighting. The only remedy that kept him going was his love for music. He had no patience whatsoever, and his students feared him not because he was bad-tempered; but they knew what music meant to him and that he would not accept less than perfect when it came to meeting his expectations.

With George, however, things were a little different. Miller treated George with respect and seemed genuinely interested in his ambitions. Maybe he was trying to fill the emptiness in him left by his son's absence; maybe he saw in him the determined young guy Howard was when he was his age. Several times after class Mr. Miller made a point to quiz George on extra work. George found this annoying at times and even complained to his mom about it, but Isabella worried that if George made a big deal out of it, Mr. Miller would fail him, and no student in the entire music department wanted to be failed by Howard Miller. George listened attentively, but was still annoyed. Undoubtedly, the teenage sentiments inside him, like that of any other youngster, made it difficult for him to see clearly.

It took Isabella many heated talks, and in some instances, tense arguments, to get this into George's brain. Even when she made sense, it still didn't seem right to him. She was afraid that by pushing him so much, Mr. Miller might cause George to abandon piano, or worse, leave the music school. Sympathizing with George, she phoned Mr. Miller to arrange a meeting with him. Two days later she went to Mr. Miller's office for a brief meeting. Mr. Miller walked in with his usual look, emotionally distressed and unhappy. Right away, Isabella felt awkward and wanted the meeting to end quickly. "Nice to meet you Mr. Miller. Isabella Khudry, George Munssif's Mother," Isabella said.

"Good Morning!" Mr. Miller replied, not saying anything else.

"Thank you for agreeing to meet with me regarding George," Isabella said.

"I understood from our phone conversation that George is having some kind of trouble with the amount of work I am giving him! Is that correct?" Mr. Miller asked.

"I believe that is true," Isabella quickly responded.

Mr. Miller showed disappointment on his face, leaning back on his chair with arrogance as if he had been personally attacked.

"Listen, Mrs. Khudry," he had a hard time pronouncing the name correctly. "I treat all my students the same. I have been in this school for many years, and I can tell when I see someone like George with such a talent and ambitions. I always try to build their confidence more, it doesn't mean I am pushing George more than any other student, but I believe he is a very bright student when talking about music."

"Thank you for your confidence in George, sir!" Isabella interrupted Mr. Miller. "Honestly, I am concerned that he might decide to give up playing piano if he feels pressured," Isabella continued.

"Now, that would be a sad thing," Mr. Miller said, picking up a pen from his desk and rolling it back and forth between his fingers.

Mr. Miller seemed to be more comfortable with Isabella after 15 minutes talking. For the first time in years he managed to show an expression of a long-forgotten smile, a success that no one had previously achieved, no matter how hard they tried. The meeting lasted well beyond the time scheduled. On her way out, Mr. Miller extended his hand to Isabella.

"Thank you for coming," he enthusiastically said, standing up from his chair.

"My pleasure and thank you for your time," Isabella replied, pleasantly satisfied.

Mr. Miller sat back in his chair, pulled out his class schedule, and flipped a couple of pages. Then, suddenly, he rushed out the door, running down the hallway to the parking lot where he caught up with Isabella.

"Pardon me Mrs. Khudry, can you do me a favor and have George either call me or stop by my office? I need to talk to him and he doesn't have class with me until next Thursday."

"Sure! I'll mention that to him as soon as I see him today," replied Isabella.

"Thank you!" Mr. Miller said, a little bewildered.

Walking back to the building, he removed the reading glasses he seldom wore outside, stuck them in his jacket's front pocket, and shook his head in disbelief (probably for doing something very unusual for him, running out of his office).

George didn't have class that morning, and waited impatiently for Isabella's return. As soon as she unlocked the door, George emerged from his room.

"Hello George," Isabella pronounced.

"Hello mom. So how was the meeting?" He calmly asked. "What did you think of Mr. Miller? Didn't you find him a little obnoxious and rude?" George continued.

Isabella moved toward Albert's chair with George following her footsteps. It was her favorite sitting place in the house. She set her handbag on the floor next to her and looked at George smiling.

"How was the meeting?" George was anxious to know.

"Fine!" Isabella said.

"What do you mean fine? What did he say?" George questioned, a little agitated.

"Mr. Miller wasn't anything like I expected," Isabella told George.

"I told you he is obnoxious and rude," George responded.

"No, I don't mean that, in fact he was very polite," Isabella abruptly interrupted George. "When we first met, he seemed worried and uneasy. Is he always like that?" Isabella wondered.

"Oh, yeah! You should see him in class. That's why no one can stand him," George replied.

"Well, he understood your concern. At first, I felt that he took it personally, but a little later he changed his attitude and was more open," Isabella explained. "By the way, he asked if you can call him or stop by his office when you're on campus," Isabella said.

"Did he say why?" George looked surprised.

"No, he didn't," Isabella replied, getting up from the chair.

"I wonder what he wants now," George said, running his fingertips on his forehead.

"I am sure you'll find out from him soon," Isabella responded, trying to reassure him.

After toying with the idea of calling or not, he decided to not call, because he wasn't ready to listen to another lecture about music. He figured he'd talk to Mr. Miller on Thursday when he sees him in class. Thursday morning George came across Howard Miller in the hallway.

"Good morning, sir," George spoke first.

"Good morning," Howard replied, looking as usual annoyed.

That was the only interaction between the two. George was surprised that Mr. Miller didn't mention anything about not calling him, and kept walking toward the classroom. Soon after he took his seat, Mr. Miller showed up with bunch of folders in his hand, set them on his desk, and proceeded immediately to passing the attendance binder. The topic for the class this morning took a different twist than the usual solely musical matters. Mr. Miller lectured about music and politics, and how the reformation of German music mirrored the complex relationship between music and politics in the 20-century Germany. Students' feelings about the topic were mixed: some were bored and others found it interesting, particularly George. He looked at Mr. Miler with attention that followed every gesture and absorbed every word spoken. He seemed more attracted to the political part of the discussion. The class lasted close to an hour and 35 minutes, well beyond the usual time allowed of an hour and 20 minutes.

"Sorry, sir, for not calling you," George said. "I got the message but decided to wait until today so we can talk. If you have some time after my next class…" George continued explaining.

"Can't do it today," Mr. Miller replied, again with his arrogant attitude. It was as if he were punishing George for not respecting his request to call him.

"That's fine, sir. Let me know when is a good time, and we can talk," George calmly said.

"Will do," Mr. Miller abruptly said.

At this point, George knew that Mr. Miller was mad as hell for not calling him, but really didn't care. He walked away and decided to skip his next class, as he felt uncomfortable coming in late. Instead, he made his way to the library. On his way, he stopped at a public phone on campus and called his mom to check in and to complain about Mr. Miller's contemptuous attitude. Isabella listened to him while he got his frustration out.

"Hey Mom," George started the conversation.

"Hi, George. Is everything okay?" Isabella replied.

"Yeah! I'm okay. Just called to check how you are doing?

"I am fine, just finished a phone interview with a hospital about a job. I am supposed to meet with them sometime next week."

"Great! I hope things will work for you," George confidently said.

"Thank you!" Isabella responded. "Tell me! How are things for you this morning at school?"

"The usual, nothing new, except today's lecture by Mr. Miller was interesting. He talked about music and politics in 19th century Germany," George explained.

"I hope you enjoyed it," Isabella said.

"Yeah, it was good," George replied.

"Did Mr. Miller talk to you?" Isabella asked,

"No, I apologized to him for not calling and explained to him why, but he gave me the cold shoulder and didn't even bother to say something," George said. "So, I decided not to bring it up to him ever again unless he says something. Listen mom, I have to run my next class is about to start, we'll talk later today when I get home. Bye!" He said this in a hurry, hanging up the phone.

At home Isabella was feeling little down, with job prospects difficult to come by. She spent weeks looking and having phone interviews, but nothing had materialized so far. She wasn't even sure if it was worth going to next week's meeting. At around 5:15 George showed up looking tired. He unlocked the door and was greeted with an appetizing aroma emanating from the kitchen; Isabella had cooked Lebanese food that had not been on the table for some time. They sat at the table. George couldn't wait to taste everything. The conversation went in many directions, life in Rochester, the years spent in Cleveland, school, Isabella's search for a job, memories from Lebanon, music, politics, and ended up with Mr. Miller. Laughter filled the room every time something funny came up. The best thing that made Isabella almost shocked with laughter was George's imitation of Howard Miller. The way he walked, talked, and especially his arrogant mood.

George joked with Isabella saying, "I wish Mr. Miller could taste this food. Maybe that would change his behavior."

"Has anyone ever told you what his problem is? He seems very disturbed," Isabella asked.

"I heard some stories around campus, but I am not sure what I heard is true," George admitted.

"What stories?" Isabella asked with interest.

"He got divorced after his son died in a car accident, and also his oldest daughter cut ties with him because she blamed him for her brother's death and the divorce," George explained.

"That's really regrettable," Isabella said, pushing her plate slightly toward the center of the table. "I had a feeling when I met him that something was not right in his life. Does his family live in town?" she asked.

"I think his wife lives on the other side of town, and I don't know about his daughter," George replied.

While George spoke about Howard Miller's life, Isabella was shaking her head feeling sadness for him. She thought about asking George to invite him to dinner one night, but having a divorced man in the house, even if George was there, would not sit well with Lebanese traditions and culture. She quickly dismissed the thought and kept silent for a moment. They both cleared the dinner table and brought tea to the living room, in keeping with the Middle Eastern tradition of sipping on a nice cup of black tea after dinner. As they sat facing each other, Isabella in her usual chair, Albert's, and George facing her on the other side leaning back on the couch with his legs crossed, the home phone rang.

"Hello!" George answered.

"Good evening George," a voice on the other end said.

"Who is this?" George asked.

"It's Mr. Miller, your professor."

"Hello, Mr. Miller," George answered, giving a surprised look to his mom.

"I hope I am not calling at the wrong time," Mr. Miller apologetically said.

"Not at all, sir," George replied in a well-mannered tone.

"Good!" Mr. Miller said.

"Is everything okay, sir?" George wondered, still looking at his mom.

"Yes, I just wanted to apologize for my behavior today with you. I know I should have been more considerate, but sometimes it is difficult to take time and think," Mr. Miller said.

George couldn't believe his ears. He made a gesture to his mom with his hand. "Not a problem sir," George said.

"Well! I guess I'll see you tomorrow in class," Mr. Miller said kindly, as if he were smiling on his side of the phone.

"I'll see you tomorrow," George replied.

"Goodbye George," Mr. Miller pronounced before hanging up the phone.

"Goodbye sir," George said, astonished.

Howard Miller was literally a man of few words. He didn't speak much and the phone conversation did not last more than few minutes.

George, still amazed by the phone call, turned to Isabella who was wondering what was going on. She knew Howard was on the phone after hearing George saying, "Hello Mr. Miller," but she didn't know why he was calling.

"What did your professor want?" she asked.

"I can't believe what I heard," George said, sitting back down.

"What? What did he say?" Isabella pressed George for a response.

"Mr. Miller has never apologized to anyone on campus, not even other faculty or management. He called me to say sorry for his behavior today. Do you believe that?" George said again, surprised.

"He's not that bad after all!" Isabella enthusiastically replied.

"I guess not!" George said.

After two cups of caffeinated tea, George didn't feel like going to sleep. For the first time he decided to pull a book out of Albert's small library. Albert was an avid reader and was interested in politics, mostly books about the Middle East and Western politics. George grabbed a book, took it to his room, laid down on the bed, and started reading it. As he flipped the pages, he became intrigued by the information in the book. He read about 30 pages before he put it down. The complex relationship between the West and the Middle East and the historical structure of the Middle East were too deep for George to fully understand. He knew from sometimes listening to his dad talk about issues ranging from the Palestinian-Israeli conflict to the Lebanese fragmented social and political structure, that these points have been the center of tension for decades, but could not understand the rationale behind all this tension. He carried that book with him every day reading few pages when he had some time between classes and at home.

Isabella noticed that George was reading Albert's books and was fine with that. In fact, she was pleased to see him getting interested in reading. The only things he ever seemed to read anymore were music notes or his school work. A couple of days later in the week, Mr. Miller happened to find George reading the book on his break and, curious, wanted to find out what he was reading. George set the book aside and got up to greet Mr. Miller.

"Hello sir," George politely said.

"Hello George, how are you?" Mr. Miller asked nicely. What are you reading there?"

"Oh! Just a book that I found at home," George answered.

"*The Tale of Two Cultures*. It's a very interesting book; I read it few years back," Mr. Miller proudly said. "I didn't know you were into politics."

"I just started reading this book," George said.

"Well, if you ever want to read more political books, let me know. I have a bunch of titles that might interest you," Mr. Miller offered.

"Thank you, sir," George replied.

"Bye now," Mr. Miller said.

George sat back reading from where he left off. He was so fascinated by the details and the events in the book that he kept reading, not paying attention to the time for his next class. He walked in five minutes late. Nancy Cook, his humanities instructor, didn't mind; she was flexible and didn't worry when students walked in a few minutes late now and then. Much like Howard Miller, she had been teaching at Eastman for years and knew the routine very well, so she didn't let it bother her too much. George gave her a quick nod to say "I am sorry for being late." She nodded back in acceptance of his apology.

While Nancy was explaining the historical conditions that led to certain African countries' underdevelopment, George was still noticeably distracted by other thoughts, scribbling a few notes on his notepad. He was recording some of the ideas he had read in *The Tale of Two Cultures* and wanted to remember. The only time he put his pen down and paid attention to what Nancy said was when she got to the role of colonialism and its long-lasting effects on those African countries.

Later that day, George finished the book at the library after school. As soon as he was done, he hurried to the political section of the library, unusual for George who usually spent hours looking, searching, and reading piano books. He pulled several books, mainly those written on terrorism and political struggle, piled them on the floor on the aisle, and started going through them one by one. Three hours later he put the books back, checking out only one. The clerk knew George, and she also knew that the only books he ever checked out were music books.

"No music books today George?" she commented.

"No, not today," George replied, handing her his student card.

"Thank you," the librarian pleasantly said.

"You're welcome," George answered.

"Here you go," the librarian said, handing George his card back and the book.

"It's due back in one month, remember," she continued.

"Yup! See ya!" George said on his way out.

Chapter 2
THE START OF THE JOURNEY

In almost a year's time, George had read every book in Albert's library at home and some more from Eastman's library. Isabella had noticed the change in George's daily routine; she didn't want to jeopardize her relationship with him, as he was drifting away from his piano passion. He didn't practice piano as he used to and didn't talk anymore about music. Isabella didn't want to stir the pot, so to speak. Now, at a little over 18 years of age, George's mind had evolved to look at things from different angle, and was seriously considering taking time off from school and finding work to help his mom. He tried to talk to Isabella about it, but she wouldn't even listen to him. No matter how hard he tried to convince her, she resisted the idea and even phoned his uncle Laurent Munssif, a well-known and respected lawyer in Lebanon, to try and talk some sense into him.

For almost two days Isabella spoke very little to George. She was very upset with him and didn't want to argue any longer about it. George, on the other hand, didn't see anything wrong with taking some time off from school. He felt the need for change because expectations from everywhere were hitting him hard—Isabella's persistence for him to succeed at school, his assumed responsibility for his own life and his mother's at an early age after his dad's passing, even Mr. Miller's expectations for him to be a great pianist. The anxiety kept inside for so long started showing up in signs of dissatisfaction. He needed to run away from all that and find something else within which to bury his sadness. The idea of leaving school and finding a job sounded like the perfect solution to him.

The quiet and happy home that Isabella had worked so hard to build had become a place of unhappiness and constant disagreement. She again thought about talking to Mr. Miller about George's decision, but decided that this was family business and should stay as such. She thought about moving again, this time to Lebanon, but what would she do there? And besides, she would never leave George alone. He was everything for her no matter how mad she was at him.

The campus library became George's second home. He spent countless hours there reading books and searching employment ads. He would come in the evening and find Isabella sitting on her chair waiting impatiently for him to walk in. She tried to hide her pain and suffering, but it showed on her face.

George would grab something to eat and sit a bit before disappearing to his room. Isabella wished so much for Albert to be around.

The end of the school year was near, and usually by this time many colleges had recruitment career events for new graduates. Eastman College was all set up with companies from the private sector, government agencies, and other universities with many open positions. George knew about the career event from his friend Larry Williams. They became friends but never truly connected deeply, perhaps because they were each in their own world and had different perspectives on life. They used to sometimes have lunch together, joke a little about Mr. Miller and discuss class materials. But, they never really built a strong bond.

Larry, unlike George, seemed less concerned with life's expectations, enjoying parties, dating here and there, acting indifferently. He was more concerned with his looks than anything else. His actions and lack of thoroughness got him in hot water many time with his teachers, the registrar's office, and even his parents, but Larry didn't really care. In one of his conversations with George he mentioned that he would rather work in the family business than be at Eastman. His parents had inherited a fortune from both their parents, and his dad had taken over his family's meat packaging business. Larry was very smart and got into Eastman not because his parents were rich, but because he was an A student. He couldn't benefit from a scholarship like George for obvious reasons, but could join

Eastman by covering all expenses which his parents agreed to pay. At first, Larry was quite immersed in his studies and very much enjoyed what he was doing, but after a few months in the program he started losing interest.

George recalled one incident between Mr. Miller and Larry that almost got Larry suspended from school. Larry did not turn in an assignment and Mr. Miller, inflexible and uneasy about everything, wasn't going to give Larry another chance. He bluntly told Larry the assignment would not be accepted and would get a failing grade. Larry flipped out on Mr. Miller, yelling, "You can't do that! I said I will turn it in tomorrow!" But Mr. Miller strictly refused and asked Larry to leave the class, which he did only after throwing his chair on the ground and slamming the door walking out. After that incident Larry was out of Mr. Miller's class for almost a week and when that happened it meant one thing only: a suspension. This strictly-enforced rule was made known to all students when they first enter Eastman. Unfortunately for Larry, he couldn't buy his way out of that one, even with his parents' money and connections.

Larry's situation put George on guard, and he kept his distance from Larry when he came back from his suspension. George could not afford any trouble and his mom was not like Larry's parents with all that money.

The career event on campus was a full-day event, packed with students trying to find out what opportunities were out there waiting for them once they graduated. George moved from one table to another looking at brochures, flyers, and general information about companies. He didn't ask any questions. He spent a good two hours at the event walking around until he stopped at one table with two young gentlemen dressed in suits and ties, both well-groomed.

"Hello," George started the conversation.

"Hello, sir. How are you today?" one of the two people at the table asked.

"Good, thank you," George replied.

No other words were spoken for close to two minutes while George was interestedly engaged in reading the information.

"Are there any questions you would like us to answer for you, sir?" The other gentleman asked in a kind of pleasant, yet serious way.

"No, thank you." George said lifting up his eye at him.

Again, George without a word walked away with some information from the table in his hand.

"Thank you for stopping by, sir. The first man who said hello pronounced.

"Bye," George kindly replied.

George left the event and headed home. When he arrived, Isabella was happy and excited. She had finally received a call from where she had interviewed, Livingston County Department of Health, Reproductive Health Center, to start working. She couldn't wait for George to get home to share the good news with him.

As soon he walked in Isabella said, "I finally got a job!"

"Really? That's great news," George responded, smiling.

"Yes, I did," Isabella continued.

"Where?" George asked.

"Livingston. It's the Department of Health."

"Congratulations! When do you start?" George enthusiastically asked.

"I don't know. They want me to come in next week to discuss the schedule and some other matters I guess," Isabella said.

Seeing Isabella so happy that she finally found a job, George didn't want to mention anything to her about the career event or his job search. The day was going just fine and there was no rush in ruining Isabella's own moment of long absent joy. He decided to wait for the right time.

Weeks went by and Isabella was enjoying her new career. Although the 20 mile commute was a drag and seemed more like hours of driving, once at work she forgot all that. She was happy just to be driving somewhere instead of aimlessly wondering around the house day in and day out. She worked very hard and her schedule shifted from one week to another, sometimes not seeing George for 24 hours. He was either asleep when she got home or she would be gone when he arrived. She no longer had to worry about him like when he was a child in Cleveland. He was a man now and could handle the responsibility of caring for himself. He filled his empty time at home without Isabella around by reading a lot. He got to the point where he could read an entire book in one day's time, most of them on politics.

Close to summer break George started sending out job applications to different places to test the waters and find out what the chances were for him to get a job. However, he received no responses to any of his applications. Isabella had no idea about George's job search; he decided not to talk to her about it for fear she would continue to disagree with him. Summer went by with Isabella working and George doing his own things, sometimes at home, other times meeting friends from campus in town. There was no trip to Lebanon that summer or any other time since George had no desire to go back, and Isabella couldn't get time off work. On her days off they spent time together mostly taking care of matters they had no time to do while Isabella was working.

The school year began, and George went back to his classes, now in his second year. No much changed on campus over the summer. Mr. Miller was still there. The librarian was still there, although she had gotten married during summer and seemed quite happy about it. People were congratulating her. One thing did strike George: Larry did not show up to any of the courses. Maybe he travelled with his parents somewhere and they were not back yet, he thought.

A few months had already gone by since the school year's beginning, and George had rarely touched the piano except during music classes. He still played very well, although he stopped practicing like he used to. Mr. Miller noticed that George was not as interested in piano, but could not tell him anything because it was none of his business what George did out of his class.

On November 16, 2003 George came home as usual, swung by the mailbox, grabbed the mail, and unlocked the front door. He then throw the pile of mail on the dining room table and proceeded to check the phone for messages, finding only Isabella's, letting him know that if he wanted to eat there is already food for him in the fridge that she cooked before going to work. George opened the fridge and pulled out a juice since he had already eaten at the cafeteria campus. He sat at the dining room table and went through the mail. It was all the usual junk, including a couple of bills, one from the dentist's office and the other from the electric company. He set them aside and continued going through the rest of the mail when he got to an envelope labeled **United States of America**. Under that in small print he noticed **Central Intelligence Agency**. He opened it very quickly, unfolded the white letter, and started reading.

Dear Mr. George Munssif,

After carefully reviewing your application, we have decided to contact you to schedule a phone interview regarding opportunities with the CIA. Please contact us at the number below with the best times we can contact you and a phone number where you can be reached.

I look forward to speaking with you in the near future.

Sincerely,

Douglas Brown,

Recruitment manager

The interview took place the following Monday as scheduled while Isabella was gone. Douglas was pleased by George's answers and asked him when he could come in to take a proficiency test to determine his skills and ability to join the Agency as an intern. George agreed to two weeks from the phone interview date. Now, the toughest thing was how to break the news to Isabella. George was embarrassed to have hidden sending applications from his mom and was mostly embarrassed because this was not what Albert and Isabella had taught him. He couldn't bear the thought of lying to his mom, so he decided to speak to her about it. Although he was 19 years old, he never lacked respect for Isabella or did or said anything that would have hurt her feelings. He had always been considerate and humble with his mom.

George waited two days before he asked Isabella if he could talk to her when she had some time. He was smart enough to pick the right time to speak to her. She agreed to speak to him right away, as she had always done. George pulled the letter slowly from the left back pocket of his khaki shorts. Khaki was his favorite color, and all of his clothes were either khaki or black. He handed the letter to his mom without saying a word. Isabella reached out, grabbed the paper, and asked, "What's this letter?"

"Open it mom, you'll see," George said with hesitation.

Isabella opened the letter and the first thing that jumped at her was the CIA seal on the letterhead. She looked up at George saying, "The CIA? What's all this about?"

She went on reading the first couple of sentences and handed the letter back to George, saying, "Are you going to explain to me what this is, George Munssif?"

"This looks to me like a job letter from the government, right?"

"Yes, it is?" she replied.

"I am sorry I never told you that I sent out applications. This is the only response I got. I also had a phone interview with the CIA," George continued.

"And where was I in all this?" Isabella said, raising her voice a little.

"I am sorry mom. I didn't talk to you about this because every time I spoke to you about finding a job you wouldn't even listen to me," George tried to explain.

"So, because I wouldn't listen, you go apply for a job with the CIA?" Isabella tensely said.

"It's not a job; it's an internship for now," George replied, trying to calm her down.

"And what's going to happen to your school and dream to be a great pianist someday? You are just giving up all that, I assume," Isabella said, raising both her hands in the air.

In the midst of the heated conversation, mainly from Isabella's side, something struck her: the person sitting across from her was no longer the little George who was running around the house making noises and playing hide and seek. He was now a man with his own ambitions and desires. Immediately, she changed her tone of voice and realized that she had to get beyond her fear of also losing George. Forcefully, she stood her ground and made George promise to finish school before he decided to pursue what he wanted. He agreed. He told her about the exam he was asked to take and she was okay with it.

Two weeks later as planned, George showed up at the CIA office ready to be tested. He was greeted by the receptionist, who showed him the way to the testing room. The room was an office with a desk, a computer, and several file cabinets stretching along the wall. After the receptionist left, he sat down, waiting for the testing people to show up. A good 20 minutes went by before a gentleman in a dark suit knocked on the door and walked in.

"You must be George?" the man questioned.

"Yes, Good morning," George replied.

"Good morning. I am Peter Whitman, the test administrator. I'll explain to you the test procedure and time in a minute, let me just login," Peter said.

When he had entered the computer's testing system, Whitman again addressed George. "The first part is composed of online multiple choice questions, which takes an hour. Then you will listen to some recordings and translate them to English, in your case from Arabic. Any questions before we start?" Peter asked.

"How much time is for the second part of the test?" George questioned.

"The translated part is not timed. Take as much time as you need to get all the three parts translated," Peter said. "If you have any question or need something just come out, my desk is right around the corner from this office."

"Thank you, sir," George said.

"Good luck George!" Peter said on his way out.

"Thank you!" George replied, already staring at the computer screen.

The test lasted almost three hours; each hour Peter came and took a quick look in the room, asking George how was everything going. The toughest part for George was translating the paragraphs from non-classical Arabic, but from some Middle Eastern Dialects. The regions that were chosen for the test were Iraq, Yemen, and Sudan. George had a hard time understanding the different pronunciations and words meanings. He did the best he could, but was disappointed because although native in Arabic, it was very different from how the Lebanese speak.

Once George was done, he made his way to Peter's desk to let him know that he was finished. Peter stood up, asking, "How was the test?"

"It was good. I am not sure about the translation part, though," George said.

"Do you have any questions for me?" Peter politely asked.

"Not really. I just want to know when I should expect to hear something back," George questioned.

"It takes about three weeks to review the answers and make a decision. We have to send your test to our headquarters in Washington, DC, and that usually takes three to four weeks to get a response back. We'll let you know when we have an answer," Peter explained.

"Sure! Thank you very much for your help," George politely said.

"My pleasure!" Peter replied.

"Take care." Peter continued shaking George's hand firmly.

George thought about the test and his answers all the way home. He was concerned that he missed more than the required points to pass, but there was nothing he could do now except to wait. Isabella was home getting ready to head out.

"How was the test?" she asked.

"It was fine. I am not sure about the translation part," George said. "I had to translate some Arabic dialects which were totally different from what we speak."

"What were the dialects?" Isabella said.

"Iraqi, Yemeni, and Sudani," George answered.

"Those are different," Isabella said, joking. "When will you hear back?"

"The test administrator said 3 to 4 weeks. They have to send my test to Washington, DC."

"I have to leave; I am already late for work. We'll talk later," Isabella said, grabbing her bag and rushing out the door.

"Bye!" George pronounced.

"Bye!" Isabella replied, closing the door.

Exhausted from his test, George stayed home the rest of the day, not doing much except going through his school homework. For a while he sat at the piano to play something. He found himself enjoying that and stayed at the keys for quite a while. Time was going by quickly, and the night started picking through the sky. Isabella had a late shift, and George was on his own for dinner. He heated up some leftovers and settled on the couch. Isabella checked in by phone at around 8:45 p.m. George got up to answer the call and knocked the plate on the floor spilling the food.

After talking to Isabella for few minutes, he rushed to the kitchen, grabbed a towel, and cleaned the mess before she got home. He knew how neat she was. She wouldn't go to work until the house was spotless and the dishes all washed and neatly arranged. That was something Albert really loved about her.

Now that Isabella had agreed that George was old enough to make his own decisions, things were much better at home, and George focused on finishing up his school as promised. With two more years of college until graduation, George focused on his studies and kept doing whatever he needed to do to graduate as planned. At the same time, several weeks had lapsed and still no response about his test results. He never talked to anybody about his test or interview with the FBI except to his mom. Even when he was going through hard times after his dad passed away, he never told anybody how he felt.

On campus, Larry was back and seemed more calm, behaving quite differently than before. He showed an appreciation for learning and was taking school seriously this time around. The days of foolishness and devil daring seemed to be behind him. No one could figure out what happened to him during the time he was gone. The rumors were that his dad met some young lady and married her after she basically wiped his fortune out, leaving Larry, his mom, and his siblings broke. Other people thought Larry finally grew up and cleaned up his act before it was too late.

George and Larry talked here and there and were a little closer since Larry came around, but a strong sense of competitiveness in class was born between the two and each one wanted to prove to the other who was better. This competitiveness was good for Larry, who deep down saw in George a good influence for success and was motivated to follow him. Their relationship grew tense as the weeks went by, however, and neither of them could stand the other to the point that they had a few serious arguments, but nothing beyond that happened.

Close to three months had now passed and still no response to George's test results. He gave up on the idea and decided to wait until he finished school at Eastman to worry about what to do next. Time was rolling quickly and spring break was couple of days away. Final exams were in full swing and George spent the week before reviewing and preparing for his tests. Everything went well. He scored very high and was pleased with his hard work.

On Thursday, April 20th, 2003 George couldn't believe that he received a letter from the CIA headquarters in Washington, DC, announcing that he passed the test and should expect a phone call to discuss the next step in the process. The phone contact followed a few days after the letter arrived. Isabella was excited but still unsure about her feelings around George's decision.

The whole thing reminded her of the time Albert worked for the CIA in Lebanon, which was why they ended up in Washington, DC and then Cleveland. His life was in danger many times. She never told George about that. The only thing George knew about his dad was that he was an architect. To that day

Isabella still believed that Albert was somehow assassinated and did not die from heart failure.

Albert joined the organization as an agent after one of his professors, himself an agent and teaching at the American University of Beirut, approached him with an offer to work for the American government. At first Albert didn't know what the work was, but soon realized that he would be working for the Agency, spying. The thought scared him, and he envisioned all kind of things happening, but took the job nevertheless. The US government suspected for a long time that terrorism from Al-Qaida and other cells was active in the region, but could not confirm it. Although Americans were operating in the country and spoke Lebanese, Albert was the right person for the job because he was a native and no one would suspect what he was doing. It was difficult for anyone to link Albert to the CIA because he didn't have the look or the personality of an agent. He was one of the natives and acted as one of them. After many discussions with his professor he accepted the job. The process was fairly simple as the Agency wanted to get someone hired as soon as possible. Within couple of months Albert was on the Agency payroll. His training was all done in Lebanon in an undisclosed location supplied by the Lebanese government and the U.S. embassy outside Beirut.

Even Isabella didn't know at that time. They were engaged and planning on marrying after college. She found out only after they got married. Albert told her the story, and although she felt little displeased with Albert at first, she didn't mind because she never tried to find out what a CIA agent's job is like. It didn't matter much to her as long as Albert was never absent.

As time went by and political tensions escalated in Lebanon, Albert was more involved with the CIA. He worked late and was gone more and more but Isabella never questioned Albert's whereabouts. She knew he wouldn't tell her even if she asked him. One early morning in 1983, Albert packed a small case with some clothes and told Isabella he had to go out of town for a meeting. To her surprise, he never mentioned anything about it the day before. Even he wasn't prepared for this sudden trip. He had received a call from someone the night before that a catastrophe was about to happen in or around Beirut. No credible intelligence was available, but whoever called Albert knew exactly what he was talking about because the very next day an attack on the Marine Barracks killed 221 American servicemen.

The tragedy was devastating not only for foreign forces, particularly Americans, but also for Lebanon's own reputation. With its geographically strategic location bordering the Mediterranean and its long-standing international recognition as the Switzerland of the Middle East, the country feared the worse, a collapse of centuries of history. Albert was one among hundred others sworn to never let that happen. He was seen by many in his work entourage as a man with a jealous disposition for his country. He felt so strongly about his views that sometimes he crossed the boundaries of the hierarchical order, which put him at odds with some of his co-workers, especially his supervisor. Neither of them was willing to accept the other, and that created an atmosphere of discomfort and hostility between the two. Jamil Chehab was a long-time FBI senior special agent who worked for years in different parts of the Middle East and South America with a sharp personality and mastery of several foreign languages. He was brought in for his expertise as a special agent in charge immediately after the Marine barracks event to oversee the investigation.

From day one, he didn't see eye-to -with Albert for no apparent reason. They just didn't hit it off, and after a couple of meetings had an exchange of short arguments about the investigation. From that time on, the two made it clear to everyone that there was no lost love between them, especially Jamil, who had the advantage of calling the shots. He went out of his way to make Albert miserable, to the point that he wanted him out of the agency. The situation lasted few months before Albert decided it was time for him to leave Lebanon. That is when he asked to be transferred and was brought to Washington, DC for training and to get him out of Jamil's sight.

It turned out later that Albert did not die from a heart problem, but was poisoned in Cleveland. Nobody could suspect who was behind Albert's death, and no test could show what had really happened despite everything that was done to find out how he died. Isabella knew that Albert was in danger even before they left Lebanon. She always worried that someone would try to get to him sooner or later, but she never thought that could happen in Cleveland, because no one knew where they lived except their families back in Lebanon. She was sure that whoever poisoned him had come from Lebanon just for that. George was in total darkness about all those events in Albert's and Isabella's lives. The only thing he knew was that Albert was an architect and died from heart problems.

Chapter 3
THE POINT OF NO RETURN

The summer started and George was all set to begin his internship in the CIA building at the Rochester Resident Agency on 100 State Street, Suite 3000 NY, 14614. After the initial orientation and a few onsite classes, George was placed in the international division to train. The division was called Squad 9, known as the Join Terrorism Task Force (JTTF). Its mission was to protect the US from terrorism and from domestic and international groups. It also worked on counterintelligence to safeguard the U.S. from foreign intelligence operations and espionage.

George's role was to provide translation and analysis of highly classified and confidential documents. The work load was heavy and George had lot to learn before he felt comfortable. His mentor Scott Conwell took good care of him and spent lot of time teaching him the ins and outs of what makes a great FBI agent. George, in following his years learning to be a great piano player, was very receptive and soaked in every piece of information and advice Scott gave him.

During those summer training months, George was gone most days, and every time he left the house Isabella felt something shocking her, sometimes to the point where she would cry. She would look at Albert's picture at home, not saying anything except taking a deep sigh as a relief from weariness. She told herself everything would be just fine. She tried so hard to overcome her sadness and to some extent her disappointment about George's decision to join the CIA, but she could hardly fight her thoughts of fear and worry that now had become her daily struggle.

Summer soon went by and George returned to Eastman for his last year. He organized his time well between his internship and school. His course load was lighter this last year, with only a few classes, mainly specialty courses in George's case: Art and Music Leadership. Nothing had changed at school, Mr. Miller crossed paths with George few times in the hallway, seeming more pleasant and calm, and Larry was still on his best behavior, staying out of trouble and seemingly committed to his studies.

With all the obligations in his life now, finishing up school, FBI training, and his mom, George still made time to stick to playing piano. He performed in several events on school campus and even performed in Merkin Concert Hall at Kaufman Center during the international yearly music concerts held in New York. Isabella could not make it to watch him this time around due to her unpredictable work schedule. He was on his own. Some of the very famous composers and music legends in the world were present and seemed completely immersed in what they were listening to. A total silence filled the concert hall with the exception of a cough here and there or someone whispering something in someone else's ear. The only sound that filled the hall and echoed from the high ceilings and walls was George's fingers on the piano keys closing with his own composed piece in memory of his father, 'The Day We Met'. He was a true virtuoso! As always, George was proud and signs of great satisfaction showed on his face as people applauded him. Mr. Miller, sitting in the front row, nodded to George with a smile as a sign of a job well done. After the concert on his way out, George was stopped by a man in his 50s who shook his hand.

"That was a great performance you did young man," the man said. "You have a lot of potential."

"Thank you, sir!" George responded.

"How long you've been playing piano?" the man asked.

"Since I was a kid," George replied.

"Good, Good! I think you have a bright future as a pianist," the man continued. "This is my card, stay in touch."

George looked at the card briefly before he stuck in his pocket. The card read *Narciso, Yepes.*

George had no idea who Yepes was. He talked to him for little while and was on his way home. He threw his bag and jacket on Isabella's favorite chair and headed to the kitchen. While he waited for the microwave to go off after he put some food in it, he pulled the business card out of his pocket and looked at it closely for few seconds then stuck it in a drawer with bunch of other cards.

Later in the evening Isabella walked in, exhausted from a long day. She found George on the computer working on CIA training materials due back later in the week. They exchanged a few words before she headed straight to her room.

George stayed up few more hours to finish his work. The documents he was reviewing varied from counterfeiting to the sale and distribution of narcotics, and some of them were on counterterrorism. For the first time he heard about words such as domestic and international terrorists groups, and FIG (Field Intelligence Group), which is a combination of CIA intelligence analysts, special agents, language analysts, and surveillance specialists. George barely knew what this all meant. This was all very foreign to him. He sat at the computer searching for more information to familiarize himself with all this new jargon he was reading. In the middle of one of the debriefings written by a senior CIA specialist he came across the words Afghanistan and Al-Qaida written in bold letters. George didn't think much about what that meant. He kept reading for a while when he realized that the time was now close to 2:00 a.m. He logged off and went to catch some sleep; he had a busy day ahead of him. As he lay looking at the ceiling, he thought about some of what he had read. The words Afghanistan and Al-Qaida remained in his mind. He now was curious to really know who Al-Qaida was. Why is Afghanistan the in U.S. government's interest? He couldn't sleep, so he got up, walked to the computer, and sat down again, searching and reading until the sun came up. Isabella stood over his head.

"Good morning, you're up early," she said.

"Good morning. I didn't sleep," George replied.

"Were you up all night?" Isabella asked.

"Yes, I had more work to do than I thought," George said.

"You're going to have a long day," Isabella commented.

"I'll come home early today and get some sleep," George answered. "What's your schedule today?"

"It should be light, but then again you never know what could come up in a hospital. Why?" Isabella questioned.

"Oh! No reason, just wondering," George replied.

"I need to get ready," Isabella said.

"Okay!" George replied.

George left the house right after Isabella. He didn't have class that morning, but had to be in the office early. Upon his arrival he found a stack of documents sitting on his desk waiting for him. He dove into the stack right away.

"Good morning. I am Silvia Thornton," a young lady walked to his office saying.

"Good morning, George Munssif."

"I heard about you," Silvia said.

"I hope good things," George joked.

"Nothing bad," Silvia replied.

"I was assigned to help you with some documents, I understand," Silvia said.

"Which department are you with?" George asked.

"I am a data analyst with the Fusion Center," Silvia replied,

"What's the Fusion Center?" George asked.

"These are centers that share information and integrate the data and evaluate its credibility. There are more than 70 centers across the country. They were created after 9/11 to improve information sharing across agencies," Silvia explained.

George listened attentively while Silvia was describing the mission of the centers. Silvia graduated from Yale University with a major in Near Eastern Languages and Civilizations and worked for a while for a nonprofit organization before she joined the FBI. She was born and raised in an upscale area of New Haven, Connecticut known as "The Hill," which is also home to Yale-New Haven Hospital and Yale School of Medicine. Silvia's parents' fortune was old money from her grandparents' involvement in the manufacturing business before it collapsed. Her father was able to hold on to the family legacy and bring it around. Despite her wealth and education, Silvia was down-to-earth and worked really hard to prove herself. Her friendly personality left an impression on anybody she came in contact with.

George was drawn to her from the first time their eyes met. He felt like he knew her all his life. Her clear complexion, green eyes, and shoulder length hair made her look younger than her age. Her unique smile radiated from her round face making visible her excitement and passion for what she did every time George asked her a work-related question. He was anxious to know everything about her and could barely stop himself from inviting her out, but he decided to wait a little longer. This was only the first day they met, and he wasn't sure what her response would be.

They both worked on those documents for the better part of the day. The afternoon was lighter with a meeting after lunch for George. Silvia left the office. They agreed to finish the work the next day. In the meeting, George listened to some interesting conversations about Afghanistan and terrorism. The round table meeting lasted two hours with CIA analysts, intelligence experts, and counter-terrorism agents participating. George took notes and translated a list of words that had to be included in a report to be sent to various Arab-speaking countries around the world.

As in any meeting with sensitive issues and where people are expected to produce quick and positive results due to the nature of the problem, tensions flared between some of analysts, intelligence experts, and counter terrorism team members, as each group had an agenda and wanted to handle the problem in accordance with the directives given by their superiors. These groups were formed to work together and coordinate their efforts, but they butted heads on where priorities were and who should be leading the operations. After all, this was in a way understandable, since the high profile issue of terrorism and terrorist groups created fierce competition throughout different secret government agencies. Recognition and prestige in solving the terrorism problem and putting an end to terrorists' activities were also at the center of that competition. George witnessed those heated arguments, but had no authority to express his thoughts; he was still an intern and didn't know which group he would end up working with.

The CIA Director, Albert White, known as A.W. in the Agency, was a demanding man who didn't like to bargain on his decisions. His own work ethics were the operating standards at the Agency. Those ethics were not always correct, but his 25 years in the military left a lasting mark on his character which was very difficult to change. Being in charge of the CIA was not an easy job. A.W. had to prove to everyone that there was only one way to do things and that was his way. Stories had it that his unfriendly and somber character caused him to lose friends and even family because of his uncompromised personality. Even at the CIA, people avoided him unless there was a reason to deal with him directly.

After 9/11, the government was desperately looking to fill positions with people who had to have one important characteristic for the job, and that was ruthlessness. Positions varied from air marshals to army soldiers and even the highest position in the CIA. A.W.'s name came up as a strong candidate from his close Army friend, Steve Dunkun, now a four star general and a member of the National Security Committee. He knew A.W. very well, as A.W. served under Steve for five years in a special force back in early 1990. They also spent some time together in Desert Storm. Steve strongly believed that if anybody could reshape the Agency to get results it would be A.W. During his confirmation hearing, three committee members, even though didn't know him, refused up front to endorse him and made that clear to him from their questions. Because others didn't really care about his personality, they were convinced he was the right guy for the job. A few weeks later A.W. was confirmed.

At that time, the country was going through chaos and finger-pointing, and a decision had to be made, even if it wasn't the right one; compromises had to be made quickly as people wanted results and it was the right moment to sell the new candidate to the American people. A.W. didn't take long before bringing on board some of his closest entourage to join the CIA. One of his retired Army friends was Douglas Green, who was now a global terrorism consultant for the Agency. His first mission was to Saudi Arabia to hold talks with the Saudi intelligence services. Douglas knew nothing about the culture nor had he ever been there. Other people from the Agency were more qualified and spoke the language, but A.W. didn't care much, he wanted loyalty. Muslims in general, and Arabs in particular, were in no mood after 9/11 to deal with ex-Army retirees, let alone a spy who had no idea about their culture. The Saudis totally discounted Douglas's presence because of his arrogant and pretentious attitude. Really frustrated from the lack of cooperation, Douglas phoned A.W. enraged.

The phone rang in A.W.'s office at 10:00 that morning. FBI director's office, Stephanie speaking," the secretary answered.

"Mr. White, please", the voice said.

"May I tell him whose calling?" The secretary asked.

"Douglas Green."

"One minute please," the secretary politely requested.

"Albert speaking," A.W. said when his secretary called.

"Mr. Green is on the line sir", Stephanie said.

"Put him through," A.W. ordered.

"Hello! Douglas here."

"What's new?" A.W. asked up front.

"These Saudis are not cooperating at all. They are a bunch of…" Douglas sounded really stressed.

"How far did you get?" A.W. asked.

"Nowhere! The only time I met with one of their people on Thursday was very brief and not much help," Douglas explained.

"No need to waste any more time there. We'll get those busters to cooperate one way or another. Call the office when you get back for a formal briefing," A.W. said before hanging up the phone.

Monday Douglas was back and immediately phoned A.W. to set up a meeting. Stephanie told him A.W. wouldn't be back until Wednesday, at which time he could meet. She jotted down the date on an open time slot for Wednesday afternoon. At 2:45 p.m. on Wednesday, Douglas walked into the office as planned, still looking exhausted from his trip to the Middle East and the pressure he was under to find some answers for A.W. Stephanie greeted him pleasantly, asking him to have a seat while she let A.W. know he was there. She walked in the office and came back. "Mr. White will see you now," she said with a smile.

"Thank you," Douglas replied, making his way into the office.

A.W. got off the phone as soon as Douglas walked in. "Good to see you Doug," as A.W. called him.

"Same here, sir," Douglas replied with a somewhat submissive tone.

"What's up with the Saudis? I thought everything was set up to talk to them before you went there," A.W. asked.

"I was told that the head of their intelligence knew about our meeting, but when I got there no one showed up. I spoke to one person who had no idea what I was talking about," Douglas explained.

"Who told you about the meeting?" A.W asked

"I got an email from the National Joint Terrorism Task Force manager," Douglas replied.

"Isn't his name Skip Hallway?" A.W. asked

"Yeah, I think that's right" Douglas responded. "What are we doing with the Saudis?" Douglas impatiently asked.

"I'll talk to Skip to find out what's on his mind," A.W. replied.

"I'll call you in day or two," A.W. added, leaning back on his chair.

Douglas got the message that A.W. wanted him to leave. He stood up, said, "Thank you for the meeting," and left.

A.W. immediately called Skip.

"Hey Skip, this is A.W." he said.

"Hey Albert," Skip was the one allowed to call him Albert. "How is it going?" Skip politely asked.

"Good!" A.W. answered.

"Douglas just left my office complaining about the Saudis not meeting with him. Do you know anything about that?" A.W. continued.

"Yeah, I do," Skip said. "I set up the meeting with the head of Saudi intelligence, but when Douglas got there, Mr. Fahd Al-Wadhihe refused to meet with him. Matter of fact, he called me while Douglas was there and complained to me about him," Skip told A.W.

"What was the problem?" A.W. asked, now curious.

"Well, Douglas was very impatient from what I understood, yelled at somebody there and used some language about Arabs that the Saudis found offensive," Skip said.

"He didn't mention anything about that," A.W. replied.

Skip was quiet, he didn't comment on A.W.'s reply. "So, what's your plan now?" A.W. asked Skip.

"We need the Saudis to cooperate. I am sure they can help figure the hell out of this mess," A.W. continued, sounding a little on edge now that Skip told him what happened with Douglas.

"I already called the Saudis' head of the intelligence and apologized to him. He understood, but also said that neither he nor any of his staff will talk to Douglas," Skip said.

"Fine. Leave Douglas out of this, and don't send him back there. Do we have anybody else to do the job?" he asked.

"I am sure we can find someone in the department who's familiar with the Middle East," Skip responded.

"Good! Then, get on it and let me know as soon you find the right person for the job," A.W. ordered. "We'll talk," he said before hanging up the phone.

Skip didn't waste any time. He got to work right away, arranging a meeting with different department heads looking for someone who could be trusted to work with the Saudis. But the fragmented structure of the Agency and the bureaucratic mindset was not something easy to overcome. It took days of memos, emails, and wasted time before Skip was finally cleared to find someone with the expertise he needed. Philip Lawson, in his late 50's with a strongly built 6'2" frame was the right person, Skip thought. He joined the agency at a young age as an intern and worked his way up to a special agent position after only a few years. He was very organized and took his work seriously, but was impatient. Philip's relationship with the Middle East went way back to his time as a teenager, when he spent several years in Saudi Arabia when his father was deployed to a U.S. military base there. He learned Arabic and continued learning the language when he joined the CIA until became fluent. One thing he could never learn was diplomacy; his trouble with his behavior of impatience and overbearing manner of dealing with people may have come from his military upbringing. He wasn't good in taking advice and was suspicious about everything around him. His time with the CIA had loosened him a bit, but didn't change him much. He stood firm for his beliefs and didn't really care what anyone else thought of him or said to him.

George did some work for him before and didn't like his style. He found him to be stubborn and difficult to get along with. But no one could do anything to discipline Philip or even fire him because they needed him to work with the Saudis and there was nobody else to do it. Philip knew that and took advantage of the situation. Internal politics in the agency had no limits. To get the job done, especially after 09/11, all bets were off, and competition and conflicts grew bigger between different groups trying to overshadow each other to find an answer to the crisis.

George was part of that and witnessed the chaos the agency was going through. His internship was ending and he was being considered for a full-time position, so in his best interest, he played his own politics by not taking sides. He did what he was assigned to do and kept his opinion to himself. He figured that keeping his nose clean was the best thing to do if he wanted to score a career position at the agency.

That didn't take long. When Philip was assigned to handle the Saudi situation, he brought George on board on a full-time basis because he was familiar with his work and was pleased by his performance. George was gratified by the opportunity, but was less enthusiastic about working for Philip.

Isabella wasn't thrilled either that George's life was fully committed to the CIA. When George broke the news of his full-time assignment to her, she didn't react. She couldn't. He seemed very happy.

Upon starting in his new position as an analyst, George was moved to Philip's department where he spent great deal of time working on intelligence information. He got to work right away. The Saudi matter was at the top of the agenda and A.W. wasn't going to allow Skip a long time before he summoned him to his office. The work load was overwhelming, and the Saudi case was much bigger for George to handle on his own than anything he had handled up to this point. Both Skip and Philip were under the gun to produce something for A.W. ASAP.

A few days later a document was handed to A.W., who immediately called for an urgent meeting with the head of Saudi intelligence, Mr. Fahd Al-Wadhine. The next day, Skip and Philip boarded a flight to Riyadh, Saudi Arabia. A.W. insisted that Skip go along. He wanted to make sure that this time around the Saudis had no complaints as they did with Douglas. He trusted Skip's judgment and felt less comfortable sending Philip alone. The Agency had already been tainted by lack of credibility, and A.W. didn't want this second chance to fail.

The Saudi authorities were already at Riyadh's airport waiting for the U.S. Secret Service arrival. The encounter was warm and yet not too friendly, since the Saudis had not forgotten what happened with Douglas before. The accusations and lack of respect weren't something easy to brush aside for the Saudis. Skip was more aware than his predecessor and showed more appreciation for the Saudi culture. Straight to a meeting with Fahd Al-Wadhine, the two entered the Saudi intelligence building accompanied by couple of Saudi agents. Fahd Al-Wadhine was pleasant and friendly.

"Nice meeting you, Mr. Wadhine," Philip said first in a clear Arabic pronunciation.

"The pleasure is all mine," Wadhine replied. "You must be Mr. Hallway? He continued, turning to Skip.

"Good to meet you, sir," Skip pronounced.

"Welcome to the Kingdom," Wadhine said. "Have a seat, please," Wadhine invited Skip and Philip.

The Saudi Secret Services had already done their homework to know who Skip and Philip were. They knew Philip spoke fluent Arabic. The meeting went well, and Mr. Wadhine seemed more inclined to listen to the American side than before. Almost three hours later, the three were still talking and throwing jokes here and there. Dinner was arranged at around 9:00 p.m. in an upscale seafood restaurant in downtown Riyadh called Al-Nafoura. The guests appreciated the addition of Western food to the Saudi menu as neither was familiar with the Saudi cuisine. Wadhine had that planned.

The discussion continued through dinner on national security, international terrorism, and Israel. The Palestinian conflict came up, which Wadhine shut down quickly. He was a smart man and did not want the discussion to deviate from the real purpose. Philip anticipated that and tried to steer the conversation in a different direction. Skip could read between the lines that the Saudis had no interest in discussing something beyond their borders. Immediately, Skip proceeded to apologize to Wadhine for Douglas's behavior, and that was very welcomed by the head of intelligence.

The dinner lasted a couple of hours, ending with a handshake and a ride to the Marriot. A follow-up meeting was set up for next day to go over some security partnership matters. In the hotel, the two did not waste any time calling A.W. for a debriefing. The time was late in the Kingdom, and a twelve hour difference was not an issue for Skip because A.W. was waiting for that phone call.

The next day the meeting started early and wrapped up around 12:15 p.m. for Skip and Philip to be at the airport for their flight back home. The Saudis and their counterparts reached some agreements, and both sides were happy with the negotiations. The one thing that was still not agreed upon was the Saudis' acceptance to allow the CIA to lead their own security operations in the Kingdom. Fahd-Al- Wadhine refused to even consider such cooperation, and the Americans were not very happy with that because after September the 11th they had carte blanche from many countries to set up secret investigation and interrogation locations. The Saudis, however, refused to play that game. Before Skip returned to Washington, the U.S. Secretary of Defense had already called the ambassador of Saudi Arabia to express the White House's discontentment with the Saudi government's lack of response to the U.S. government proposition to operate in the Kingdom.

Back at the Agency, work was in full swing trying to coordinate full-scale operations in countries from Somalia to North Africa and parts of the Middle East to find and dismantle any organization suspected of terrorism or supporting terrorist activities. The Saudis' involvement with the U.S. was already deep. With over thirty thousand soldiers in the Kingdom and other U.S. civil contractors, accepting the intelligence domination would have put the country at a higher risk of political unease and social confusion. Mr. Al-Wadhine was smart enough to realize that the potential for unrest was far greater than the benefit of the CIA help.

The U.S. government however, decided to deal with the Saudi objection differently. The Agency figured the only way to have a watchful eye in the Kingdom was to go beyond the agreed-upon accords. The Agency turned to its trained personal in the Middle East to assemble a group of agent experts in Saudi dialect and familiar with the Saudi culture. The Agency even hired outside people for their mission. George, in his third year with the Agency, was one of the people considered for this illegal intrusion. A list of names was quickly put together and given to A.W. for approval. Upon receiving A.W.'s signature, Skip started calling the people on the list one by one for an interview. George was the last one to be called. On Monday morning at around 9:45 a.m., he walked to Skip's office. He didn't have to wait; the secretary was made aware by Skip to let him in as soon as she showed up.

He knocked on the door lightly. "Come in," he heard Skip's voice saying.

"Good morning, sir," George politely said.

"Good morning, George," Skip replied, standing up from behind his desk to shake George's hand. "How are you?" he continued.

"Fine! Thank you," George said, looking a little intimidated.

"Have a seat, please," Skip offered.

George sat down on the edge of the chair. "Thank you, sir," he replied.

"You must be wondering why you are here?" Skip asked.

"Yes, I am," George said.

Skip smiled. "I'll get straight to the point about why I contacted you for this meeting," he said. "The Agency is looking for qualified and committed agents to take care of some business in the Middle East. We have already put together a list of potential people who we feel can do the job. Your name was also included," Skip explained. "I know that you have been with the Agency for a little over three years working as an analyst, and that you are fluent in Arabic. We are interested in agents who speak Arabic. I will give you an idea about the nature of the work involved in a minute."

George listened attentively to Skip speaking. He nodded his head often in agreement with Skip, but kept silent. About 45 minutes later the meeting was interrupted by a phone call that Skip answered.

"Hello," Skip answered, reaching for the receiver very quickly after one ring only, sounding as if he was bothered by this unexpected call.

"Hello, A.W. here. How is it going?"

"Hello sir," Skip replied

"Where are we with the Saudis? I signed off on the list, how far did you get?" A.W. asked.

"I am working on it and will have something for you very soon," Skip replied.

"Let me know when you come up with something," A.W. asked in an authoritative tone.

"Will do," Skip replied, and hung up the receiver.

"Sorry about that," Skip apologized to George.

"No problem," George replied.

The meeting went on for about two hours with Skip explaining to George the details of the mission. He did not press him for an answer right away. He asked him to take a day or two to think about it and get back to him with a response. George agreed.

After George left Skip's office he went back to work thinking about Skip's offer. He was excited about the opportunity, but at the same time it triggered fearful thoughts of the unknown. This isn't going to be an easy decision, he thought.

He needed to talk to someone; he needed to share his thoughts with someone. This time around it was Silvia Thornton. She was smart and could help him figure things out. George wasn't looking for approval, he was able to think clearly, but he needed that extra mind to help sort things out. Isabella was too emotional and he could not talk to her without having her break into tears.

He phoned Silvia and asked if he could meet with her to talk. She accepted. They arranged to meet after work in a small café called *Café Fato*, Italian for *destiny*. The owner, Alberta Conti, an Italian lady in her late 60s from Sicily, had run the café for over 20 years with her son, Alvise Conti, a 30-year-old with an overweight build from all the pasta he ate. His loud voice could be heard from the kitchen sometimes yelling in Italian, but when Alberta spoke, he was like a baby trying to win his mom's satisfaction.

Alberta wasn't just any woman; she had been through a lot in her life. She lost her husband Calvino right after coming to America during a holdup in a convenience store; her eldest daughter Carina had a failed marriage after 15 years when her husband was found guilty and condemned to 35 years in jail for money laundering and possession of drugs. Carina moved on with her life and was now living in a Washington, DC suburb working as a sales rep for a cosmetics company. She was really good at what she did and was doing really well for herself. She went to visit Italy whenever she had a chance. The Conti family still had relatives in Sicily and they enjoyed visiting each other during vacations and holidays.

Alvise decided to stay with his mom to help her with the café. Alberta needed the help. She wasn't young anymore, and besides, she wanted Alvise to be in charge in case something happened to her. Alberta loved people and was very warm. She fed anybody that walked into her place and if they couldn't pay, she used to joke with them saying, "Remember me if one day the table turns around." She grew up poor and knew what being hungry meant. One day she got really mad at Alvise and even told him that maybe he should leave the café and not come back because he kicked a homeless man out. Café Fato was a small place with bright colors and checker drapes covering the bottom half of the windows. Tables were neatly scattered around the place, with small Italian handcrafted porcelain vases and a fresh rose in each vase. Alberta didn't care much for paper napkins; she insisted that each customer have a linen napkin. She wanted her customers to feel at home when they walked in. Alberto's husband, Calvino, loved listening to Andrea Bocelli; that was the only music Alberta played in her place.

George and Silvia met at the café around 4:45 p.m. Alberta knew George. He was a regular, and Alberta liked him because she found him polite and well-mannered. A few times they had talked about leaving their countries and coming to the U.S. She liked him because they had something in common; both were away from home and related in some way to each other. Italians and Arabs have much in common in traditions and way of life. George was almost Alvise's age. Alberta considered George as a family member and greeted him with warmth every time he showed up. Even Alvise was comfortable around him making jokes. One time as soon George walked in Alvise yelled, "Look who's here—the Lebanese!" George just smiled and grabbed a seat. Alvise walked from around the counter and shook George's hand.

"Good to see you man!" he warmly greeted George.

George and Silvia sat at one of the tables. When Alberta saw them she came running.

"Hi George!" she announced.

George stood up, took few steps toward her and gave her a hug. "Good to see you, Mama Alberta," George said. Most customers called her Mama Alberta.

"This is Silvia. This is Mama Alberta," George introduced them to each other.

She shook Silvia's hand. "Nice to meet you darling," she said. "So, when is the wedding? I'll be looking for an invitation," Alberta joked, cracking up. She was a very direct person and said what she felt, even if sometimes some people didn't care much for her jokes.

Silvia blushed with a grin on her face. George put his head down, a little shy and embarrassed. He quickly changed the subject, asking Silvia what she wanted to drink.

"A cappuccino will be fine," she requested.

"Two cappuccinos, Mama Alberta, please," George asked.

"Go sit down. I'll bring them to you," Alberta offered.

Alberta disappeared for a little while and came back with the cappuccinos and two pieces of freshly made tiramisu. She made all the pastries herself. "Little something from me to you two. Enjoy!" She set everything on the square, burgundy, linen-covered table.

"Thanks, Ms. Conti," Silvia politely said.

Alberta wished so much that her son would meet someone like Silvia. She wanted him to settle down before something happened to her. At least she would be happy knowing that she hadn't left him alone. Alvise and his sister didn't have a close relationship. In fact, they hadn't spoken for few years because of family disagreements. Alberta more-or-less sided with Alvise, which made Carina move away and even cut all ties with her mom for quite some time. Alvise's life, on the other hand, was much easier than that of his sister with her failed marriage, her relationship with her family, and her nature as a very tense Italian woman who wanted everything to go her way. That is, in part, why she didn't get along with her mom and brother. Alvise's only worry was a good poker game and his favorite homemade dish of *spaghetti all'marticiana.* He never thought about marriage and wasn't the type of person to go home after a long and tiring work day. With few friends, he spent almost every night playing poker until late into the night. He enjoyed that life style and wasn't ready to explain his actions and decisions to someone else. Alberta was the only person with that authority. Looking at George and Silvia, Alberta felt little envious. She wanted her son to be like George. George and Silvia seemed so connected.

They sat across from each other, Silvia leaning back on the chair and George with his arms folded in front of him on the table. He kept looking at Silvia the whole time while speaking. He asked if she liked working for the Agency and if she had plans to do something else in the future. Silvia knew exactly what she wanted, but didn't totally open up to George. She needed more time to know George and to share with him her life's details. George understood that.

"Thank you for accepting the invitation to meet with me," George respectfully said. "I just wanted to get your opinion on something," he added.

"Sure!" Silvia quickly answered.

"I had a meeting this morning with Skip. You know Skip right?" George asked.

"I heard about him, but never actually met him," Silvia replied. "Isn't he the head of the National Joint Terrorism Task Force?" she asked.

"Correct!" George replied. "Anyway, he called me today and asked if I was interested in taking an assignment overseas. I am totally unsure of what to do," George said.

"Where overseas?" Silvia seemed curious to know.

"The Middle East," George replied.

"You mean Saudi Arabia," Silvia responded.

"Do you know about Saudi Arabia?" George asked, surprised.

"This is not new. They had this issue with the Saudis not cooperating for quite some time, and the difference has never been resolved. I worked on several files regarding this matter," Silvia explained.

George listened to every word Silvia said. He was glad that Silvia was there.

"So, what did you decide? Is this something that interests you?" She asked.

"I really don't know. It sounds like a great opportunity but I am not sure what to do," George commented.

"The Agency and the Saudi Secret Services have been at odds for a long time and some agents have been really frustrated by the situation. Some blamed the Agency for lack of proper training and communication," Silvia added.

"You mean they already sent people there before?" George asked.

"Oh, yeah! On many occasions, and nothing was done. The other problem is that some agents didn't feel comfortable working closely with the Saudis, and the Saudis similarly didn't trust the Agency," Silvia replied. The conversation went on for a while before they decided to leave Café Fato. Silvia never told George what he wanted to hear: Take the offer or turn it down. She was careful enough to let him think things through on his own and decide what's good for him.

Outside the café, George offered to accompany Silvia to her car. It was dark and sometimes that part of town got a little rowdy, but she elegantly declined saying "I'll be fine. My car is just around the corner."

George sensed that Silvia was too prudent to rush into a relationship. She had already experienced a failed relationship, which taught her to be more cautious. She had been engaged to wed a man whom she met in a state-wide government sponsored expo event and who worked for a state environmental agency, but was never interested in making it a career. Once she found out the guy was only interested in her father's fortune, the wedding was called off.

She walked away smiling at George, while he stood there waiting for her to disappear around the corner. She was gone. George could barely stop himself from following her, but he patiently waited for the right time. He got home later than his usual time; Isabella was already there waiting and worrying as usual.

"Hi, George!" she enthusiastically announced, sitting on her favorite chair, holding her reading glasses in one hand and a medical report in the other.

"Hi, Mom!" George replied, scratching his forehead. "What a day!" he continued.

"Did something happen?" Isabella curiously asked.

"No, just busy," George said.

"How is work?" Isabella asked, trying to initiate a conversation with George.

"It's fine," George replied. "What are you reading there?" he asked.

"Oh, this? It's just a patient medical report," she replied.

"I might be travelling overseas for an assignment," George suddenly announced to Isabella.

"Where to?" Isabella asked with a disagreeable tone.

"To Saudi Arabia," George said.

"What's there?" Isabella asked.

"There are some disagreements with the Saudi authorities that need to be worked out, and Skip asked if I could travel there to attend a meeting," George explained. He was very careful choosing his words. He intentionally didn't say Saudi Secret Services because he knew she wouldn't like the sound of that. Despite George making it sound like a regular business trip, Isabella didn't look very excited and wanted George to reconsider the assignment. She could not force him not to go, but she wanted him to know that she wasn't thrilled.

"When are you leaving?" she asked.

"I don't know yet. I had a meeting with Skip and he asked if I was interested," George replied. "I'll probably know more about it once I let him know my decision," he continued.

For a few days George didn't bring up the subject again, but that's all there was on Isabella's mind as George had noticed from her behavior and hinting here and there during their evening conversations. "How is work?" she would ask.

George skillfully downplayed Isabella's curiosity and always gave the answer she was looking for in a very settled and yet diplomatic way. "Work is fine, everyday something new to learn," he would say to her.

"Did you decide on the Saudi meeting yet?" she asked.

"Yes, I think I am going," he told her. "This is a good experience for me and I want to see what happens in these kinds of meetings," he explained.

Isabella looked at him and didn't say anything. George could sense that her mind wasn't on reviewing her hospital reports; she would jot down a couple of comments on one of the reports, look up, and then look down at the report again. That's not the way she usually does things, he thought to himself. When she reads, not just reports but anything for that matter, she gets totally consumed by what she is doing. This time she was not that same person. George didn't ask any questions. He said good night and walked away.

Isabella sat in Albert's chair and for a long time inhabited another world. She would sometimes shed tears and other times smile to herself. Maybe she was shedding tears because she was silently complaining to Albert; maybe she was smiling because she wished that Albert was there to see his grown up son going out to the world. She finally stood up, set the papers aside, and turned the lights off on her way to her room.

A week later, George, Skip, and Philip were at JFK airport waiting for a flight to London and from there to Riyadh,

Saudi Arabia. British Airways flight 105 was on time. All three boarded the plane and settled down for the seven hour journey across the Atlantic. It was great weather to fly, sunny and warm with no major prediction of weather changes. The takeoff was as normal as any other flight, with the aircraft climbing, then smoothing into the sky and disappearing into the clouds.

Meanwhile, back on the ground at JFK the situation was total chaos. Fire trucks and police cars, both marked and unmarked, with lights flashing and sirens blaring, raced toward the landing strip. Nobody knew what was going on. At JFK anything could happen at any time. Suddenly flight 105 surfaced from the sky making its way back to the airport. Upon landing it was surrounded by all kind of government agencies and media stations. Later that afternoon the news reported that it turned out to be that a couple of radios surprisingly made their way into one of the luggage undetected by the highly sophisticated scanners. The only way that airport security knew about the incident is through a passenger overhearing someone saying on the phone, "I put the radios in the suitcase with all the other stuff."

By the time that passenger reported the incident and security was alerted the plane was already gone. It was contacted in midair and ordered to return. The plane sat on the tarmac for almost two hours with sniffing dogs going in and out and agents hovering around looking for anything suspicious. Finally, the decision was made to unload all luggage and rescan it all again.

The suitcase with the radios was found and the owner escorted in a police car back to the airport for interrogation.

George, Skip, and Philip waited patiently like everybody else. Three and half hours later the plane was back in the air heading to London, but without the radios in the luggage. The three arrived at Heathrow Airport too late to make the only connecting flight for the day to Riyadh. Skip made a few calls and was able to find available rooms at the Ramada Hotel Heathrow about 2 miles from the airport. The shuttle picked them up at 1:45 p.m., all three travelers were exhausted from the night's ordeal. They went straight to their rooms.

Later that evening they met for dinner, an informal meeting between the three colleagues. The discussion centered mainly around work and their meeting with the Saudis. That was new for George so he kept mostly quiet, listening attentively. Skip would glance at George from time to time, George shaking his head in agreement with Skip's ideas.

At one point Skip out of nowhere asked George if he wanted to open the meeting with the Saudis, but George declined the offer saying, "I am not sure, since this is my first meeting with them."

Skip was a bright person and knew exactly why he would want George to open the meeting. He figured George was Lebanese, and that could be the ticket to a successful meeting if he made the Saudis comfortable from the start. Philip, on the other hand, seemed a little agitated and selfish, as he loved to be in the spotlight of every event, especially high profile ones.

The next morning at 8:00 a.m., all three headed to the airport and boarded a plane for Saudi Arabia. They arrived in the capital, Riyadh, well before the time the meeting was scheduled. A Lincoln Town Car driven by a young man in a suit and tie was waiting for them. The Saudi driver spoke perfect English; he was born in the States and later moved back to Riyadh.

Back at the office, the head of the Saudi Intelligence, Fahd Al-Wadhine, hadn't yet arrived. They were greeted with drinks, coffee, tea, and sodas. George gratefully accepted the coffee. Saudi coffee was not for the faint of heart. The beverage is so strong that one can barely swallow it. George was familiar with it from his trips to Lebanon and didn't mind it.

The wait lasted quite some time, which Philip didn't appreciate. Fahd finally showed up looking exhausted. He walked in, apologized for the delay, and shook hands with Skip first, then George and Philip, and invited the three to his office. He had a personal demeanor that showed superiority and self-importance. In the office, they sat down with Fahd looking at George particularly; Skip noticed this immediately and said, "George is one of ours at the Agency."

"Nice to meet you George," Fahd replied.

"The pleasure is all mine," said George in Arabic.

"Are you Palestinian or Lebanese?" Fahd asked.

"Lebanese, sir," George politely replied.

The look on Fahd's face was little discomforting as George extended his hand. The Saudi intelligence chief did not show any enthusiasm about George being from an Arab country, which George sensed from the minute he met Fahd. But George wanted to give him the benefit of the doubt, thinking that maybe they just met and the protocol needed to be professional.

The discussion opened up with some casual conversation about their trip. Fahd listened, trying to play the great host; however, his mind seemed too busy to really be interested in the conversation about the trip. Skip, on the other hand, seemed to enjoy the not-so business-like interaction. This was unusual for the American way of doing business: very disciplined and time conscious, with a "get it done" attitude. Fahd knew all that from living in the U.S. and didn't mind. In fact, he cut the interaction very short and went straight to business.

"Did those of you at the Agency think about what we discussed in our last meeting?" Fahd asked, putting Skip in a tight spot.

Skip's long experience at the Agency taught him the art of negotiations and how to play the game with the Saudis. He knew exactly what to say. "It took us a long time to figure things out, and we had to really make compromises, but we think we came up with a compromise that I am sure will benefit both of our agencies, "Skip explained. The idea was to let the Saudis think they were in charge while the Americans ran the operations with undercover agents, but Skip was not about to reveal the real intention behind the deal.

He played his hand well and almost convinced Fahd to accept the proposition. After a long talk with much back and forth on the details of the newly proposed plan, at around 2:00 p.m. Fahd offered to break for lunch. He had a reservation at one of Riyadh's upscale hotels called Mena Hotel Riyadh. The restaurant, though not fancy, had an inviting feeling, clean with its dark wood tables and chairs. The space was nicely appointed. Its tables with white, soft silk napkins, place mats, and shiny clean glasses showed simplicity with a level of elegance. It was Fahd's favorite place; he ate there at least three to four times a month. The Euro-Middle Eastern menu had something for everyone. The conversation from the office continued at the restaurant. George looked around in admiration of the restaurant's contemporary layout, while Philip kept a close watch on everything that was said, paying particular attention to Fahd's comments. The food was served and everybody seemed to be enjoying their time, when Skip's cell phone rang. Nobody knew where he was except Albert White, the FBI Director.

Skip looked at the number on the screen before answering the call. The word *private* showed on the screen. Skip decided to answer it anyway.

"Hello Skip Hallway speaking," he said.

No answer. He said hello a couple of times and hung up.

"Sorry!" he apologized to Fahd and the others. "Must be a wrong number I guess."

The phone rang again. "Hello this is Skip," he answered with an annoyed tone.

"Mr. Hallway," an unrecognized voice said.

"Who is this?" Skip asked.

"It's not important who this is," the voice replied.

"How did you get this phone number?" Skip asked furiously.

"Don't interrupt me and listen," the voice ordered. "I have a message for you," the voice said.

Skip listened without saying anything.

"You and your agents must leave the Kingdom in the next 24 hours or else!" the strange voice continued, then hung up abruptly.

Skip got back to the table looking uncomfortable and somewhat angry, which Fahd, George and Philip clearly noticed. Skip didn't say anything. He wanted to talk to Fahd about the phone call, but wanted to do so privately. After lunch, the four left the restaurant, and on the way out Skip approached and requested if they could meet in Fahd's office later that day. Fahd agreed.

The time was 4:45 p.m. when Skip showed up for the meeting. Fahd was still in the office. He walked in, sat down and immediately asked if Fahd could put a trace on the strange phone call he received while in the restaurant. Fahd responded, "I don't think it's a problem as long as the call came in from inside the Kingdom."

"Nobody knows my cell phone number here. Even in the U.S. only a few people have the number," Skip explained.

"What's going on?" Fahd asked.

"I received a call saying I have to leave the Kingdom in the next 24 hours or else," Skip continued.

Fahd listened without responding, leaning back on his chair. Skip's story reminded him of his own experience receiving a similar call threatening his life for working with U.S. intelligence. That day he looked exhausted when he came to the office, late for his meeting with Skip. He understood what Skip was going through and also knew that the call came from inside the Kingdom.

He had traced the call that came to him to a local business run by a group of Yemenis. The business owner was arrested and his three associates were freed for lack of sufficient evidence. The business owner, named Fahmi Akram, was arrested because he hired some illegal immigrants to work in his business. This was enough for Fahd to make a case and to hold him, hoping he would get something out of him regarding the phone call. The ultimatum paid off after questioning. Fahd told Akram either he would cooperate, or no one would get him out of 20 years of jail, and maybe more, for breaking the Kingdom's laws and hiring illegals. Fahd could do it; he was not joking.

Akram knew Fahd was serious and that he'd better start talking. Akram proceed to explain that two men walked into his business and offered him $50,000 in cash if he agreed to rent them a small space in his business to run their international money transit operations. They claimed it was a legitimate business, much like Western Union. Akram agreed, and they set up shop in his business for monthly rent plus fees.

He continued explaining that he had not seen anything abnormal. For the first few months the two men ran their business. They were both there all the time. People, mostly foreigners working in the Kingdom, showed up all day long wiring money to their families overseas. They were dressed in western clothes and behaved normally, although perhaps more westernized than Arabs.

Akram said, "Then, for three or four days in a row, the same people showed up with someone I saw for the first time. He was tall with dark skin. One very distinctive thing about him that stayed with me until this day— he looked very upset. When they introduced him to me, he didn't say a word. He nodded his head, followed with a brief look at me, before he turned around and started walking away."

Akram continued, "He came back twice, as far I know, and both times he was carrying what looked like a briefcase. He hurried inside and stayed for a while before leaving. The second time I tried to find out what he was doing by walking in on him in the office, pretending I didn't know someone was there. The door was locked. I turned the knob couple of times but no one answered. I walked back when I saw the door unlock and the same guy coming out holding his brief case. He didn't say anything, walked by me and disappeared in a rush. I went to the office where he was and found a bunch of used phone cards on the desk.

"My curiosity pushed me to dig into the drawers to see if I could find anything about the guy—who he was and what he was doing with the door locked. In one of the drawers I found a piece of paper with some names, one of them Fahd Al-Wadhine. I didn't think much of that, guessing that name was a business contact."

Fahd listened as Akram went on with the details. He knew he'd get his man when the right time came. For now, he wanted to hear everything Akram knew. After almost two hours of questioning, Fahd told Akram he could leave, but he gave him a mission. He wanted Akram to find a way to bring the man to his business. Fahd didn't care how Akram did it. He was setting up a trap to lure the man into Akram's business and nab him.

"As soon as you get hold of him and arrange for a time for him let me know," Fahd ordered.

"Yes, sir!" Akram replied.

"Remember, don't try anything funny. I will have you gone before you know what hit you. Do you understand?" Fahd said authoritatively.

"Yes, sir," Akram responded, fearing what could happen to him.

"Here is my card with my direct number," Fahd offered.

Akram extended his hand to accept the card and took a quick glance at it. His eyes stuck out and his jaw dropped. Looking up at Fahd, he realized he was talking to the same "Fahd" he saw on the paper he found in the drawer. Fahd knew that Akram recognized the name, but played it down, acting like nothing happened.

"You can leave now," Fahd said.

"Okay!" Akram replied.

Chapter 4
BEYOND THE BORDERS

Skip, George, and Philip were still in the Kingdom trying to work out the agreement details with Fahd. Skip decided that an anonymous phone call wasn't going to deter him from his mission. He didn't mention anything to George or Philip; he wanted to keep the focus on the objective of the trip and not create any unwanted attention.

Skip felt comfortable, now that Fahd was on the case. He trusted his judgment and was convinced that he would get to the bottom of it.

George's time with Skip was worthwhile, as he saw firsthand how high powered negotiations, especially those relating to national security, are conducted. He learned a lot on his trip and took advantage of his familiarity with both U.S. and Arab cultures. He fit in both, and that motivated Skip to bring George close in to the action.

Philip, on the other hand, despite being quite sagacious, didn't have the required patience. His attitude of "get it done now" did not click with the Saudi mentality and didn't give him any leverage. For that reason, Skip kept him at a distance most of the time. His expertise in the Middle East was the only reason Skip took him along on this trip.

Back in the U.S., Isabella was doing fine, being busy at work along with worrying about George. Although he checked in with her from time to time by phone, she couldn't help but to worry about him. Every time he called her, she asked when he was getting back. He reassured her that everything was going well and that he should be back once his work was done.

Two weeks went by in the Kingdom and no final deal between the two agencies was in sight. Both Fahd and Skip each saw things differently. They agreed on the principles of the contract, which was a joint venture in the decision making, but the fundamental point of who would run the operation was still not clear. They ended the discussion by setting up another meeting a few months later.

One thing was still on Skip's mind, the anonymous phone call he received. He wanted to get that resolved before he left, but Fahd told him that he would stay on it and let him know when something came up. Skip was fine with that. A couple of days later all three, Skip, George, and Philip, were at the airport heading back home. Only once they reached mid-air did Skip tell George about the phone call he received in Saudi Arabia. George couldn't help but ask the obvious question.

"Why didn't you say anything back in the Kingdom?" he asked.

"I didn't think that was the right place or time to bring it up," Skip replied. "We had too much going on, and I didn't want to create a diversion from the main objective of our trip," he explained.

"I understand," George said, satisfied by Skip's response. "Does Philip know anything about this?" he asked.

"No, I don't think Philip will react calmly to this," Skip said. "He tends to overreact quickly."

"So, what was the phone call about?" George asked, curious.

"Whoever called asked that we leave the Kingdom in 24 hours or else," Skip said.

"What did he mean by 'or else'?" George continued.

"No idea what he meant by that," Skip replied. "Anyway, Fahd is handling the situation, and I should know more about this when he calls me."

Isabella was thrilled to see George after his few weeks of absence. She wanted to know everything about his trip. She kept asking him all kind of questions. In reality, she wasn't very interested in knowing the details about his work, but was just pleased to see him in front of her.

The next day in the office, Skip had a meeting arranged with Albert White for a briefing on what happened in Saudi Arabia. A.W. was not very happy with Fahd. He expected the Saudis to be more receptive, but when Skip mentioned that there is another meeting in few months, A.W. was more open to further talks. Skip also brought up the phone call he received, which A.W. saw as an opportunity to press the Saudis to accept the CIA's offer to lead the security operations in the Kingdom.

"This sounds good. I didn't think of it that way," Skip commented.

"We need to take advantage of every opportunity possible, even if it's a threat to give the Saudis something to think about. And the phone call sounds to me like a good bait," A.W. explained.

"On the same subject, I think for the next meeting we should have George lead it, based on his background. That could also work to our benefit," Skip suggested.

"That's good. You can arrange for that," A.W. offered.

George was in a full swing with the Agency now. He was handling some of the most high profile National Security dossiers in the CIA's history, such as Operation Dust in Iraq. Operation Dust was the new name the U.S. government gave to its initiative to uproot Saddam from power after U.S. policy makers failed to reach an agreement with the Iraq leader to allow the U.S. market expansion to Iraq. The intention was to start with Iraq as the hub for U.S. business ventures and from there make their way to other neighboring countries like Iran.

This was only one reason for the operation. The other and stronger motive was to contain Iran. The U.S. saw Saddam as the "bad boy" of the region. He was the only one who could control Iran, since he held power for 30 years in mostly Shia-populated country.

The plan didn't sit well with Saddam; pouring money into his country and taking over didn't sound like a good idea to him. He knew that agreeing to the plan would eventually backfire on him by isolating him from power and bringing in someone else to protect the U.S.'s interests in the region. He refused. The U.S. delegation he met with at the time didn't do an effective job of selling him their ideas. Even their offer for him to be on the CIA's payroll was not worth his time.

When all plans failed, the U.S. administration concluded that a plot to overthrow the Iraqi regime was the only option left. The CIA came up with the story of WMD and sent inspectors to investigate. The effort was led by both the CIA and a former commander of the Iraqi Special Forces who had been recruited by the CIA, who later defected outside Iraq. The goal was that the more the inspectors discovered, the stronger the case for the U.S. to justify a military invasion. The plot was a success, and the U.S. administration convinced other nations to join in attacking Iraq. The Iraqi regime was now dissolved, and the country was under siege.

Operation Torpedo in Afghanistan was an entirely different series of events. This was the culmination of years of planning to beat the Soviets in nuclear weapons capabilities by helping the Taliban drive Soviet troops out of Afghanistan. The CIA supported the Taliban with weapons and money before turning their back on them as the result of the attack that took place in East Africa and in which Bin Laden was the primary suspect. The U.S. needed the Taliban to cooperate on the Bin Laden case, which the Taliban refused to do. That refusal did not go unnoticed, and an embargo against Afghanistan was the first step of a plan that would lead to an invasion. The Taliban not only refused to hand Bin Laden to the U.S., they offered him refuge in Afghanistan. September 11th was the final straw for Operation Torpedo, giving the U.S. the needed reason to invade Afghanistan. At that time, the country now known as Russia was not very pleased, not because the Taliban meant something to the Russian regime or because Afghanistan was a close ally to Russia, but because Russia was in control of almost all oil and gas reserves in central Asia, and the U.S. government was hard at work to change all that.

The CIA had every detail of both operations, and George had access to all of it. As an analyst, part of his job was to consolidate all top secret information concerning Iraq into reports, and translate them into in English, Arabic, and Pashto. He learned this new language at the Agency. Although Arabic and Pashto have nothing in common as languages, they share the same Arabic alphabets, which made it easy for George to pick it up the language.

Growing up with Albert and Isabella, it was expected that George would be a high achiever. The CIA work made him more disciplined. He knew that he was up against people like A.W., Skip, Philip and others, and any negligence would cost him his career. So, George was now tested again with the Saudi deal. Skip was convinced he'd pull it through with Fahd. He called George to his office and asked him how he felt about leading the negotiations with the Saudis. However, Skip didn't directly offer him the mission; he wanted to first find out how comfortable George was the responsibility. They met on Monday in Skip's office.

"What did you think of our last meeting with Fahd?" Skip opened the conversation with George.

"I was quite surprised by his personality," George said. "He seemed very determined on certain aspects of the negotiations," he continued.

"You think there might be a way for us to change that?" Skip asked.

"This could be a very difficult situation to change," George commented. "I strongly believe that he will not accept what we are offering, but things could change."

"Do you think another meeting is worth the trouble?" Skip asked.

"Certainly, we have nothing to lose," George replied.

"Are you willing to head the next meeting?" Skip offered.

"I don't have a problem with that," George enthusiastically replied.

"Philip won't be there, and I might come along just as an advisor," Skip said.

Skip didn't give George details as to why Philip would not be at the meeting, but George was smart enough to know that if Philip went, he might just torpedo the whole meeting.

"I understand," George replied. "What ever happened with that anonymous phone call you received? Did you hear back from Fahd?"

"No, nothing yet. In fact, I will call Fahd to finalize the meeting schedule and at the same time ask about that," Skip replied. "I will let you know once I have the meeting details."

"Sounds good!" George replied, and stood up, ready to leave.

"Talk to you later!" Skip pronounced.

"Thanks!" George replied on his way out.

George was looking forward to the opportunity to head the mission and got back to Skip with his acceptance in a very short time. Skip was pleased and the next day phoned Fahd to set up the meeting. Fahd was not there, so he left a message to get back to him. A few days went by, and no call came in from Fahd. A week later Fahd called, apologizing to Skip for not returning his phone call right away. He said he was out of the country, but he gave no details.

It turned out that Fahd was in Pakistan, as the CIA's tracking reports showed. The Saudis were not the only ones doing their homework regarding their counterparts—so was the CIA. The details about Fahd's trip to Pakistan came from the Pakistani Inter-services Intelligence (ISI). The yearly U.S. financial aid to the Pakistani army had a purpose; it wasn't out of kindness, but a payroll. As soon as Fahd left Pakistan, the CIA was well aware of his journey there and what went on in his meeting with the ISI. Skip had all the details. The phone conversation between Skip and Fahd was casual and focused mainly on their next meeting and the anonymous phone call.

"Would two weeks from now work to meet?" Skip asked.

"That will be what day?" Fahd replied.

"Let me check the calendar," Skip offered.

There was a minute or so of silence.

"Tuesday the 19th," Skip said.

"That will work because Monday would have been impossible," Fahd replied.

"George will be there on Tuesday," Skip announced.

"Sure! I look forward to our meeting," Fahd replied.

"Will you be coming with George?" Fahd asked.

"I might. If I can free myself from other things, I will," Skip explained. "By the way, any news about the phone call?"

"Yes! We did track the phone call. We'll discuss it next time we meet," Fahd suggested.

A couple of days later, Skip send an email to A.W. with the final decision on George as the new negotiator with the Saudis, which A.W. approved and send back to Skip. The one thing A.W. was adamant about was that Skip attend the meeting as well. He needed assurance that everything would go well.

On Monday, October 18th, both Skip and George were on their way to meet Fahd. Tuesday morning they arrived in the Kingdom, ready to finalize the deal. The driver sent by Fahd picked them up at the airport. Fahd met with them at the office, asking the usual questions about the trip. The official meeting began with George now in direct contact with Fahd. Skip said very little, while George explained to Fahd the agreement details. He spoke in English so Skip wouldn't feel left out. Fahd listened to George and agreed with most of what he heard. Still, he wasn't sure about a joint venture with the CIA.

Then George unexpectedly said, "We're okay to provide the training and you run all operations."

Fahd smiled at this.

Skip, however, looked at George in dismay. He wasn't expecting George to concede so easily. Still, he kept silent.

The three shook hands and agreed to draft the final agreement to be implemented as soon as possible.

"I need to talk to you about the phone call," Fahd said to Skip. He didn't know if George knew about the story.

"Any news?" Skip asked.

"We can talk. George is already aware of it," Skip continued.

"Well! In that case, we tracked the phone call, as I mentioned, and we know who made it and from where. We are still investigating the case, but we have a pretty clear idea about the man who made the call."

"How did he get my cell number?" Skip asked.

"That part we have not figured out yet, but I am sure we'll know very soon."

George and Skip left the meeting and headed to the hotel. Skip was a little annoyed, and asked George what he was thinking to have made such a deal.

"For Fahd this is a matter of pride, and unless we let him be in charge, he won't agree to what we are proposing," George explained.

"He wants to call the shots," George continued. "I don't think we would have had any chance to win this argument with Fahd. I think we did the right thing leaving the door open for future talks." George proposed.

Skip turned over George's strategy in his head and it made sense to him. George's thinking was not very different from what Skip planned. Let the Saudis think they are in charge while the CIA secret agents did what they needed to do in the Kingdom. This seemed the logical way to get the job done.

Emails went out that same day to the CIA headquarters, one of them to A.W. letting him know that a final deal had been reached with the Saudis. Another went to Philip Lawson, directing him to draft the agreement, both in English and Arabic, to be emailed back to Skip within 24 hours. The Saudis were also drafting their own agreement, both in English and Arabic. The agreement was to be signed by A.W. Because of the nature of the deal, Skip was not in a position to approve such contract.

The same week, A.W. was on a flight to Riyadh. He met with the Saudi minister of Defense, and under tight security from both sides the deal was signed and sealed at the headquarters of the Saudi Intelligence Services. A.W.'s trip lasted for one day only. Not long after the papers were signed, CIA agents were deployed to the Kingdom and set up shop at the Saudi Intelligence Services building.

At first, things seemed to work just fine and each group had a defined agenda on what to do. However, reality soon set in, and clashes over priorities started surfacing as members of each agency had different priorities. George was one of the agents sent for a period of six month to direct U.S. agents and to make sure that the cooperation between the Saudi agents and U.S. agents didn't run into any conflicts.

Isabella was in no way supportive of George spending six months with the Secret Services in the Kingdom. She even got into a heated argument with him before he left, but couldn't convince him otherwise. Deep down, she understood that George was not a kid anymore and had the right to decide what was good for him. But every time he brought up the word CIA, she lost control of her emotions because of what happened to his dad. They worked on their differences, and she pretended to be okay with him going.

His job in the Kingdom was not easy. He had to adjust to a new way of thinking and doing things. Although he was familiar with some of the culture, he still had to make concessions in many situations not to overstep the boundaries. He had to keep both sides happy, the Saudi Secret Services on one hand and the CIA on the other, and that necessitated tact and diplomacy, at which George was very skilled. On one occasion, he got into a heated argument with a Saudi agent because the Saudi was less than inclined toward working with Americans. He made it clear to George that the American way of doing business was not welcomed by all Saudis, and that he had no interest in learning from the Americans.

Not everybody at the Saudi Secret Services knew George's background. They thought he was another American coming to tell them how to do things. George never made it a priority to tell them who he really was, a Lebanese American. Although he spoke to them in Arabic with a Lebanese accent, they still thought he was another American CIA agent who learned Arabic at the Agency.

The first few months were challenging ones, and tensions were often high, with both partners running into an obvious yet unseen hostility and an intense antagonism around this matter of national pride. George played that game well. In meetings with

CIA agents, he often hinted to them to be more understanding of the culture and not to take certain conflicts as personal. He did the same thing with Saudi agents at every chance he got to talk to them. He wanted the Saudis to also understand that this was strictly business. But for George this was easier said than done. It would take a great deal of compromise from the Americans to prove to the Saudis that this was not an open invitation to the Kingdom, and that they not only needed to be less invasive, they also needed to get out as soon as the contract expired.

Skip received weekly reports from George via email updating him on the work progress. The report was sent every Saturday or Sunday for Skip to read on Monday, but Skip never waited that long. As soon as email came in, he was all over it. Occasionally, George would mention to him in the report that opposing principles of some agents from both agencies was causing friction. This was something that Skip expected, as he had no doubt problems between the two would sooner or later surface, which was why he suggested George lead the mission.

In his email responses to George, he would reply, "We need to be sure to behave within reason there." George knew what Skip meant: Don't make the same mistake as Douglas Green.

But even with the tense relationship, progress was made. The forced collaboration led to the dismantling of a few potential incidents in the Kingdom, other parts of the Middle East and North Africa. The CIA's reach was beyond the Kingdom. The

Agency already had operations in many countries, and those operations intensified after the unforgettable events of September 11th. During the time he spent in the Kingdom, George took a few trips to Africa and Eastern Europe. The CIA, with the consent of some Africa and Eastern European countries, had established secret centers to monitor suspicious activities, sometimes going beyond what was agreed upon between those countries and the U.S. government. The CIA would even monitor governments of those countries in some instances. George knew all that and could not do anything about it. He was assigned a mission and had to live by the rules.

Once, while Skip was in Saudi Arabia to meet with George at the request of A.W. to check in person how things were going in the Kingdom, George asked Skip, "Why are we monitoring governments of some of these countries? Is this right?"

Skip looked at George and asked, "Do you realize the magnitude of what happened during that morning of September 11, 2001?"

"And who doesn't?" George quickly replied.

"Let me tell you something that no one else knows, aside from a very few people at the Agency. Consider it classified information," Skip said. "After September 11th, the rule of cooperation between the U.S. and other nations changed. The U.S. lost all faith and trust in many other countries, especially those in the Middle East. I think the feeling was mutual."

"The U.S. government looked at every foreign government as a potential threat. Not because the U.S. government was out to get some of the Middle East countries, but because over 3,000 innocent American people died in a single day from an unexpected attack." Skip kept explaining with an unusually angry look.

George, with his armed crossed, listened, not saying anything.

"We had to put all emotions aside and look at what happened to the U.S. from a selfish stance," Skip added.

"Besides, some of those countries—mainly Eastern European ones—owed us, because we helped them for long time with their political reforms. It was in their best interest to cooperate," Skip said.

"Some Middle Eastern countries, however, were less inclined, making it difficult for us to do our job. When we realized that working with some of them was going to be difficult, the only two options were either to pour billions of dollars into their economies or declare war against them, which we decided was more risky in the long run for the world's stability. Buying them off was a safer bet," Skip explained.

George's mission in Saudi Arabia took him to other locations; Yemen was on the top of the list. The U.S. Embassy in Yemen was unlike any other place. Housed in an old and renovated building, the gates were specially designed and shipped from the U.S. Barricades built of metal and square boxes set on the road on the curb lined up, one behind the other, stretching the length of almost two blocks. In front of the entrance, three U.S. marines stood straight, as if they were chained to the wall, looking at everyone who walked by and every car that drove by without even turning their heads. The high powered rifle ready to be fired looked even more intimidating. When George showed up one morning for a meeting with the U.S. and Yemeni governments, he spent close to an hour answering questions even though his badge clearly read *Data Analyst*, and in bold letters, **CIA.**

It took several phone calls, background checks, and what seemed like an indefinite wait before he was allowed in. It turned out one of those phone calls was all the way to Skip, as George would later learn directly from his boss.

George started experiencing signs of stress and fatigue as he got more involved with his work. Travelling to different locations, he seldom found time to call Isabella twice a week. He now phoned her once a month to say hello. There wasn't much to the conversations. She would try to ask him questions about his life, work and when he thought he'd be back home, and he would only tell her, "As soon as the project is over."

She would tell him, "I love you and stay safe," before she hung up. Isabella was now head of the Gynecology Department and happy with her work. She would sometimes feel alone without George, but her busy work schedule and her research helped her ease that loneliness a bit.

Every time George talked to Isabella and hung up the phone he thought about Albert and what would he say if he saw George doing what he did. Would he be happy and proud or would he be disappointed that George gave up the dream of becoming a world-famous pianist? The thought was difficult for George to answer.

He would from time to time think about Silvia and wished she was close by for comfort and to help him overcome some of life's realities. He called her only once after he arrived in the Kingdom, but she didn't answer the phone, and he didn't leave a voicemail. He needed some time to sort out his emotions.

Six months later, George was still in the Kingdom. His trip had been extended due to new security problems that the CIA became aware of. He wasn't very excited about the idea of staying longer, not knowing when he would go back. He didn't mind living in Saudi Arabia, but wanted to be back in the U.S.

During the time he worked in Saudi Arabia, Isabella visited him once, and they enjoyed their time together. George even offered for her to stay with him until they both returned to the States, but she told him she couldn't leave her work and patients for that long. She spent 10 days with him before she returned. One evening after dinner when talking to George about his job with the CIA, Isabella decided George must know the truth about his father. Somehow, George was not surprised. It all made sense now. The time George spent with his mom affected him in such way that he wanted to return to the States very soon. He felt that he abandoned her. Additionally, he was exhausted from travelling around the region.

But the situation became even more difficult for George when he received an email from Skip asking to get ready for a trip to Pakistan for talks between the CIA and the SIS. The Saudi Secret Services were a part of those talks, headed by Fahd. But this time the game changed, and George's mission had changed too. He was no longer going to Pakistan as a data analyst or even as a negotiator. He was officially spying on the SIS on behalf of the CIA. No one knew about this sudden change, not even the Saudis. This was classified information.

A week after George received the call from Skip, he was on a plane from Riyadh to Islamabad. He arrived at the Pakistani capital, where another American CIA agent by the name of Rupert De Paz was waiting. A former police officer from New Jersey, De Paz joined the CIA after 20 years as a cop with a reputation of corruption, extortion, and intimidation after he was let go from the department. Nobody knew how he made it to the CIA. Rumor had it that he falsified documents to clear his name and wipe out any records of his past activities.

Rupert had a distinct scar on his upper lip which he tried to hide by growing a moustache. It resulted from back when he was a ruthless and remorseless cop, which the CIA considered a plus for the mission. Also, his look resembled the locals very much. With black hair, brown eyes, and dark brown skin, he could easily be from the region. He even spoke the local language with a very minimal accent. He had been in Pakistan for a little over two years.

He greeted George, who had no idea who Rupert was. To this point, nobody had told him what the plan was. All he knew was to deploy to Pakistan and then learn the details of his mission. Rupert rushed him into one of the van cabs waiting on the curb. These van cabs usually wait until they squeeze as many people as they can carry before they drive away. Rupert spoke to the driver in Urdu and soon the driver pulled away from the curb with just the two of them inside.

The destination was the International Exhibit Center that housed companies from all over the world promoting their products for not only Pakistani business people, but other countries as well. Rupert, up in the cab, spoke to George in English, as he didn't want to raise any suspicion with the driver. Everyone in Pakistan knew about the IEC, and people from all over the world came to the center looking for business deals. It was a safe location to visit. Or so George thought.

The blast was so loud that it shattered the standing booths into tiny pieces and threw the display products into the air. Glass debris from the huge roof came flying down, hitting everything and everybody on the ground. This was George's first encounter with a blast. It scared him to the point that he hid behind a metal panel that was used as a wall behind one of the booths to hide some merchandise. Rupert, on the other hand, was nowhere to be seen. George's luggage was still sitting on the ground covered with dust and pieces of glass. Some Pakistani cops rushed to the luggage looking at it with suspicion while George from a distance looked helplessly at his luggage being examined by the Pakistani police.

"Grab that luggage!" one of police officer ordered another policeman.

As soon as the policeman reached down to grab the suitcase, George stormed out from behind the metal wall.

"That's my bag!" he shouted.

"Who are you?" The police officer asked rudely.

"I am George Munssif, a businessman from the U.S." George replied.

"Why is your suitcase here?" the officer asked.

"I didn't have time to go to the hotel; I had to meet some business associates here" George replied.

"Which hotel are you staying in?" The officer asked curiously.

"The Islamabad Marriott Hotel" he answered.

George had a reservation at the hotel that was made from California by a non-existent trade corporation the CIA established. California was chosen to eliminate any suspicion that George had any ties with the east coast, where the bulk of the U.S. federal government is located. A.W. and Skip wanted to play it safe, issuing George's passport, residence address, and corporation information from California. The corporation had everything legitimately credentialed: name, building address, registration with local and state authorities.

"What is your job?" the officer angrily asked.

"I told you, I am a businessman," George replied, annoyed.

"What kind of businessman?" The officer insisted in broken English.

"I am a distributor for a medical supply company in California, and I came here to talk to some people about setting up a manufacturing branch in Islamabad," George raised his voice, waving his hand while speaking as a sign of dissatisfaction.

"Is this your first time in Pakistan?" the officer asked.

"Yes," George replied.

"Do you know anybody in Pakistan?" the officer further interrogated.

"No, I am supposed to meet some business people here," George explained.

"Did you see what happened here? I mean the explosion," the officer asked.

"No, I was walking around waiting for the people I had a meeting with to show up, when I heard this loud noise. So, I hid behind this metal wall."

"Can I see your papers? I mean passport and your ticket." The officer continued pressing George for answers.

Here we go, George thought as he stuck his hand in his inside jacket pocket. George's passport read:

George Munssif

Address: 1521 Alameda Avenue, San Jose, California

Date of Issuance: 14 November 2002

Expiration Date: 14 November 2012

Place of Birth: Lebanon

Citizenship: U.S.A.

The officer looked at the documents closely for few minutes, flipping the passport pages back and forth and checking the arrival and departure information on the tickets.

"Is there a problem with the documents, sir?" George asked.

The officer was silent for couple of minutes before handing George back his papers and asked him to wait a few minutes until he got back. George remained, himself and his luggage still surrounded by three Pakistani policemen. It was almost half an hour before he showed up again.

"How long am I staying here officer?" George asked.

"You can go, but leave us your hotel address and phone number in case we need to speak to you again," the officer said.

"How about my luggage?" George continued.

"You can take it," the officer responded.

George grabbed his suitcase and headed to the exit, making his way through all the mess in the structure. As soon as he stepped outside, a hand reached him and pulled him from the right shoulder. He thought the officer must have changed his mind and wanted to ask more questions or maybe take him to the police station. He turned to find Rupert.

"They gave you a heck of a time," Rupert jokingly said.

"Where were you?" George asked.

"I saw two guys exiting the Center after the blast. They seemed in a hurry so I followed them, but it turned out they were part of a business group. They all met outside the Center" Rupert explained. "I was getting back inside, and when I saw the cops. I stood back to avoid any problems."

"What happened with them?" Rupert questioned.

"They wanted to know everything about me and why I was in the Center. What a bunch of idiots!" George said.

"Where to now?" George wanted to know.

"Take a cab and go to your hotel. You will be followed," Rupert said.

"We'll be in touch."

George hopped in a cab heading to the hotel. A few minutes into the drive, George noticed that he was being followed by an unmarked car. He asked the driver, who spoke some English, to take a turn on a narrow street. The street was paved, but had no signs and was lined with abandoned trash from vegetable merchants. The only exit from the street was maneuvering through hundreds of wooden crates piled up on both sides of the street. The driver argued that it wasn't the right way to the hotel, but George insisted and the cab turned. The driver didn't have any problem avoiding that mess. Once out, George asked the cab driver to continue driving to the hotel.

The upset driver looked at George in the rear view mirror and said, "There will be extra charge for the turn we made. It's going to make the drive longer." The driver could make up any price he wanted because there were no fare meters in the cab for George to make a case for an argument.

"Okay!" George smilingly nodded his head in acceptance.

At the hotel, George's room was ready. After he filled out the guest form, he took his key and headed to the second floor, room 228. The room overlooked a busy street, which George didn't mind as he was used to living in New York and then Saudi Arabia, where noise was a welcome sign of life and energy. The room had a western feel, with a king sized bed and matching night stands. Across from the bed a five-foot-long dresser covered the wall, with a brass lamp on one side and couple of glasses and bottle of mineral water neatly arranged on the other side. The small size TV set right in the middle of the dresser with the remote. George threw it on the bed when he realized after trying twice that the remote control was useless with dead batteries.

He flipped the TV manually, and there it was, the explosion in the Center making headline news in several channels. The hotel had a satellite dish with limited access to a variety of channels. The Urdu language didn't make it easy for George to understand what was going on. He flipped to CNN, but the Pakistani translator was speaking at the same time as the CNN anchor, so he gave up and turned the TV off. While George finally decided to unpack his suitcase, the room phone rang.

"Hello" George answered.

"Mr. Munssif, you have a call," the front desk clerk politely replied. "Do you want me to put it through?"

"Who is it?" George was curious.

"He didn't give his name, sir."

"Sure, go ahead."

"Thank you, sir," the clerk said before transferring the call.

"This is George," he said with a calm and yet a firm voice.

"It's Rupert, when can we meet?"

"Why? What's going on?" George asked.

"I can't discuss this over the phone," Rupert announced.

"Where do you want to meet?" George asked.

"Take a cab and have him drop you at the Center. Try to ditch the two guys waiting for you outside the hotel," Rupert said.

George glanced out the window but didn't see anybody. "Where are they?" he asked.

"They are at the lobby lounge, sitting to the right facing the entrance."

"What time at the Center?" George confirmed with Rupert.

"Can you make it in an hour? I don't have much time," Rupert asked.

"I'll see you at the Center in an hour," George replied.

George emptied his brief case and stuffed all his documents in his jacket pockets; he figured he needed to be light and ready in case of an unplanned event. He made his way downstairs, looking straight at the lounge entrance. He walked to the lounge and sat at a table, ordering tea, holding the dessert menu, and looking out of the corner of his eye at the two casually dressed, mustached gentlemen who pretended not to pay attention to George. They kept speaking in Urdu while keeping a close watch on George.

George signaled the waiter standing right next to the double swinging kitchen doors with his hands behind his back.

"Hello, sir," the young, dark-skinned waiter said.

"What kind of dessert is this?" George asked.

"It's a house specialty: Thin dough filled with almond and pistachio, fried and then drizzled with a mixture of honey and rose water," the waiter explained.

"It sounds great," George replied, listening to the waiter describing the dessert.

"I think I'll take one of those, and can I get some more tea please?" George requested smiling.

"Sure, sir," the waiter responded before disappearing like lightening.

A few minutes later, the waiter showed up with George's order, set it on the table, and walked away.

George took few bites and finished the remaining of his second tea cup before he got up and walked to the front desk. The two gentlemen also got up and followed George's lead. They stopped when they saw George at the front desk, one of them pretending to answer his cell phone while the other waited. George spoke to the clerk for couple of minutes and made his way back upstairs. The guys immediately went to the clerk, flashed their badges, and asked him what George said.

He said, "He is going to sleep and doesn't want to be bothered and not to transfer any phone calls to him," the clerk explained with fear.

"They looked at each other, stuck their badges back in their front shirt pockets, and proceeded toward the hotel entrance.

"Hello, sir. He didn't leave the hotel," one of them said, calling from his phone. "What do you want us to do?"

"Stay there and keep an eye on him," replied the voice on the other end of the line.

"Understood, sir," the same agent replied.

George walked to his room, flipped the No Not Disturb sign on the outside and took the back stairs leading to the fire exit. He crossed the back courtyard, looking behind his back until he was clear. He walked few feet down the street, waved to a cab, jumped in, and told the driver, "The International Exhibit Center."

The Center was still a mess from the outside, nothing cleaned, with two guards standing in front of a yellow tape blocking the entrance. A sign written both in English and Urdu was posted that read "Center Closed".

George got out of the cab on the opposite side from the Center. Rupert walked very close to him and in a low voice said, "Follow me." At the top of the street around the corner from the Center, Rupert walked into a building that had no sign or name. It was a plain building with an old staircase, half of the metal banisters missing, and only one light bulb shining, barely giving enough light to walk up the stairs. They both walked at a steady speed, making their way to the second floor of the building. Rupert pushed a door open, followed by George. The room had a few taped boxes tucked in a corner, a metal file cabinet on the adjacent side of the door, and a table set in the center of the room with four chairs.

Both George and Rupert stood in the room when George anxiously asked Rupert, "Why are we here?"

"This is the safest place for both of us for now," Rupert replied, looking out the small window by barely removing the piece of cloth covering it.

"What do you mean, the safest place and for now?" George asked, not really understanding what Rupert meant.

"I hope you realize that you are faced with two problems, the Pakistani Intelligence Services and Al-Qaida," Rupert explained.

"Is there something I don't know? And who sent you to the airport to meet me, anyway? Nobody told me about you." George started getting little irritated.

"This is the CIA, my friend. Sharing information is not the Agency's strong suit, and you know that," Rupert replied.

"Who sent me is not important," Rupert continued.

"What is important is that we are both into this, and unless we cooperate with each other, we will both be jailed for life or most likely killed," Rupert said this with a serious look on his face.

"So, why are we here?" George asked.

"The Pakistani Intelligence Services are smarter than we think. They have been dealing with the problem of terrorism for so long that they know things about which the Agency has no idea. Something else: they don't want anybody from the outside to come here and tell them what to do. Two CIA agents were shot dead and no one knows what exactly happened. The SIS is saying it was Al-Qaida, but others seem to believe it was an SIS job," Rupert explained.

"How did you end up here and what is your mission?" George asked.

"I was sent just like you. I was told you'll be in Pakistan next week, no details, no connection here. The only advantage that I had was I spoke the language," Rupert replied.

"How long have you been with the Agency?" George asked.

"Couple of years before I ended up sent to this hole," Rupert responded.

"Who do you know at the agency?" George asked, not quite comfortable with Rupert.

"Scott Conwell and Philip Lawson are the only two people I know."

Those names were enough for George to feel little more relaxed toward Rupert. "Do you know Skip Hallway?" George further asked.

"Isn't he the NJTTF manager?" Rupert asked.

"Yes!" George said.

"I heard about him," Rupert replied. "The Agency is so messed up...you don't know who is who or who reports to whom."

George didn't respond to that. He was still unsure if saying something to Rupert would come back to bite him later. He preferred to just listen. "You still haven't told me why we're here and whose place is this," George asked.

"This is our secret meeting place for now," Report responded.

"What do you mean, our secret place for now?" George asked.

"This building belongs to a Pakistani CIA informant. The Agency rents it from him under an assumed name. It's never been used for anything. From time to time agents use it for meetings when something comes up," Rupert explained. "But the building was owned by the CIA." Rupert for some reason was not telling George the truth; George could sense that Rupert was making up the story of the Pakistani man.

"And why are we here?" George pressed Rupert.

"There seems to be, according to some classified information, plans to attack the US embassy in the next few days, and we need to move quickly to prevent it from happening," Rupert said.

"Where did you get this information?" George asked.

"Sorry, can't tell you right now. What I can say, however, is that this is a credible source that has been working for us for some time and we have no reason to doubt it."

Turning, Rupert went on. "The building has several rooms and even an underground prison holding station that the CIA used for interrogation."

"Has the CIA ever held anybody here?" George asked, curious.

Several times," Rupert commented.

"Does the Pakistani government know about this location?" George asked.

"In a way they do, since they are the ones handing us over those we are after," Rupert said.

There was one location in the building Rupert didn't mention to George. They walked by a double door that looked like an entrance to a fort. The doors were made of steel. George asked Rupert, "What's behind those doors?" but Rupert played a deaf ear and did not respond.

He kept talking about the Pakistanis and how they are not in a place to control the situation without the help of the U.S. George didn't insist; he figured if Rupert dodged the question, he meant to do it for some reason. The two spent some time in the building before Rupert said, "We need to get out of here before somebody shows up."

"I thought you said nobody comes in here. George commented.

"Well, nobody except our own. And I don't want anybody to suspect anything. Some agents are not very good communicators. It's better if we're not seen together," Rupert explained.

George didn't understand what Rupert was trying to say. Some things didn't make sense to him, but he did not want to rush searching for the real story. On the way out of the building Rupert took a quick look at his watch and said, "Later!" to George, rushing out while George was still making his way towards the exit.

After meeting with Rupert, George did not go back to the hotel. Instead, he decided to take a tour of the city. He stopped in couple of shops and then walked through an open air market with restaurants and shops. He stopped at one of the tea shops, ordered a tea, paid for it. The tea was too hot for him to finish, so he took few sips and put the rest of it in a garbage container. The owner of the shop noticed that and looked offended, thinking his tea was not good enough for George. George sensed the vendor's feeling of disappointment, and to reassure him that there was no problem with the tea, he gave him a thumb up and then left him some extra change as a tip.

George was in a totally different world: nothing looked familiar to him, people and streets were unfamiliar, and he asked himself what he was doing in this foreign land. Thinking of Isabella, he had a feeling of guilt. Although he kept in touch with her, it wasn't as frequent as it used to be. His mission was too demanding, and being in Pakistan, he understood that he could be watched by anyone, and that could put her in danger even thousands of miles away. George had no idea how long he was going to be there for.

Skip knew of everything that was going on with George in Pakistan, not necessarily from George himself, and not even from Rupert, as Skip didn't really care for him. He knew his background and from day one didn't really feel good about him.

As he walked alone through the city, George asked himself if joining the Agency was a good idea. Being in Pakistan awakened in him a fear that he never knew in the U.S. or even in Saudi Arabia. He thought about his father, Albert, and what he would have done if he were here.

The Pakistani government kept a close watch on George after the international exhibit center bombing. SIS agents followed George and even checked his hotel room when he was out. They couldn't find anything. They wanted very badly to find something against him that would give them a reason to arrest him, but George was very smart and knew that he was walking on a very thin line in Pakistan, so the smallest mistake would cost him dearly—maybe even his life. He played it very safe.

Rupert was very cheap and loved money. He would do anything for money. Even after joining the Agency he was still doing some illegal deals. Many times while as a cop he would give information to mafia bosses and gang members that the authorities had under surveillance in exchange for large sums of money. That behavior stayed with him even when he joined the Agency. He didn't do it as often now, but he would not pass up a deal if he knew that it would make him money.

The Pakistanis had tested him earlier against two ISI agents who were selling information to the CIA. He accepted money from the ISI, and in return he set up the agents, who were arrested, convicted for the treasonous act of selling classified information to the CIA. Both were sentenced to be executed before their sentence was commuted from death to life in prison for unknown reasons.

Rupert, although investigated by the CIA, was never brought to justice or even a court hearing. ISI made sure to keep his records clean in case they needed him for future operations. Despite the fact that the CIA had strong evidence against him, they could not get the Pakistani Secret Services to cooperate. ISI made up a story of a former retired agent named Khan Nazir Omair, who was hired as an undercover agent to expose the two agents for selling highly classified information. Khan Nazir had never been found, and no records showed that he ever existed. ISI knew that Rupert was talking to George and that he was the only one who could get close to him, so once again the ISI called on Rupert to get in George's head. However, the deal this time was not money, but blackmail. The ISI held Rupert by the neck. Their message was either you do it or we'll make a case against you and turn you over to the CIA. A case against him means we'll find something just like they did with Khan Nazir.

Rupert had no choice. He accepted. A few days later, he met with two ISI agents to get the details of his mission. The agents explained to Rupert that they needed everything he could find out about George. "Who is he, what is he doing in Pakistan, and who are his contacts?" Rupert did not know who George was, but he knew why he was in Pakistan and who some of his contacts were (Skip was one), but didn't want to say anything. Now the game had changed, and this was not about other agents anymore. His life was on the line. His years on the streets in New Jersey and dealing with cops, gangs, and mafia bosses taught him how to navigate turbulent waters. He accepted the deal from the Pakistanis, but also, George had an exit plan.

This time around he didn't call George at the hotel; he went to the hotel looking for him. Plain clothes agents were watching the hotel entrance, and Rupert noticed them, but acted very casual. Walking to the reception desk, he spoke to the clerk in Urdu, asking if George Munssif was there.

"I haven't seen him today," the clerk responded.

"Can you ring his room for me?" Rupert asked, always in Urdu.

"Sure!" The clerk replied.

The phone rang few times, no answer.

"Thank you!" Rupert said. "I'll wait, and maybe he'll show up."

"I'll let him know that you are waiting for him if I see him," the clerk offered.

Rupert walked to the window, checking if the plain clothes agents were still there.

They were.

He stayed in the hotel lobby for 30 minutes and then decided to leave. "I'll come back!" he kind of shouted to the clerk from a distance and disappeared before the clerk could even answer.

George did not show up to the hotel for days, and no one knew what happened to him, not even the ISI. Five days after his walk in the market, there was still no sign of him. He disappeared into the thin air without leaving any trace. George had had nowhere to turn, so he contacted Skip from a private cell phone provided by the CIA to agents on missions abroad. He wanted to find out what to do and who was this guy Rupert?

Skip told George to get out of hotel and go to a safe house, to which he gave him directions. Only a few people knew about the so-called safe house, and Skip was one of them. When George called Skip, Skip didn't gave him too many details, just ordered him to leave the hotel and stay put until he heard from him. That's what George did for five days, staying in the safe house.

The safe house was on the outskirts of Islamabad in a village called Rumli. The house sat on a corner of the main road leading to Islamabad. Nothing in particular stood out about it, old as it was and looking in need of a major renovation. Walls were cracked and the roof was overtaken by moss and other debris. The intention was to keep it that way, to not attract any unwanted interest from the locals or anyone else.

The interior had three rooms and one bathroom. The inside was not any better than the outside. Although the dark colored bed looked in a good shape, the doors were missing handles and seemed to have not been cleaned for years. The kitchen was small with few cabinets hanging on one wall. The counter was long enough to have a sink on one side and a stove on the other side. Parts of the fridge at the bottom were rusted, and the motor made a loud noise every so often, as if it were an airplane taking off.

George didn't mind any of that. He felt more secure in this house than in the hotel. After five days in the safe house, he started getting impatient from loneliness and not knowing what was happening in Islamabad. He considered contacting Rupert for a minute, but decided that was neither a good idea nor a safe one. The sixth day George decided to go by himself to see if he could find any information at his hotel. Disguised in Pakistani clothes he found in the safe house, probably from previous covert operations, he caught a bus ride to town and walked into the hotel, heading directly toward the front desk.

The clerk recognized him and joked. "Hello, sir! You look good in Pakistani clothes."

"Thank you!" George replied, in no mood for jokes. "Did I get any message or phone calls?" George asked quickly.

"No messages, but someone came looking for you few days ago," the clerk said.

"Did he say who he was?" George asked impatiently. "What did he look like?"

"He was average height with a mustache, and I noticed a scar on his upper lip," the clerk explained.

George knew immediately it was Rupert. "Did he say what he wanted?"

"No, sir. He asked about you, waited for some time, and then left," the clerk replied.

"Thank you!" George said.

He took few steps toward the stairs heading to his room, then stopped and turned around. "Excuse me," he said to the clerk, "Can I get my bill? I am checking out right now. I'll be right down."

He ran upstairs and looked around the room to see if there were any cameras or microphones. Nothing. He pulled the articles he had left in the room before he disappeared for the safe house, mainly clothes. He picked what he needed and left the rest, and paid for his room in cash to leave no trace of credit cards and exited the hotel.

Outside, a black car was parked with three people sitting inside. George kept walking, disguised in his Pakistani clothes so they couldn't tell who he was. However, one of them smelled something unusual. Why would a Pakistani person walk into this hotel empty handed and come out with a small case? He jumped out of the car saying to the other two, "I'll be right back." He went to the front desk, flashed his badge in the clerk's face, and said, "Who was that person wearing local clothes who just left?"

"Which person?" the clerk innocently replied.

"The guy with the small suitcase in his hand!" His voice became more agitated and unhappy with the clerk's response.

"Oh! That was one of our guests at the hotel who just checked out," the clerk explained.

"What was his name?" The agent's voice still sounded still unhappy.

"George Munssif, why?" the clerk said.

"Damn!" the agent muttered, running back to the car. "Let's go find him!" he shouted.

"Find who?" the other two agents asked.

"The American took off; he was disguised in Pakistani clothes and just checked out," he replied.

They drove around for a while, but George was gone. He took his clothes from the case, stuffed them into a plastic bag he purchased from vendor, and ditched the suitcase in a garbage bin on the side of the road. He went to the building where he and Rupert had the first meeting. He hoped Rupert, for some strange and unexpected reason, might be there. His hand rested on his gun, ready to react if anything happened. Checking one room after another, he found nothing but abandoned paper cups on a round table surrounded by some metal chairs.

Some activity has been happening here, he thought. He found a spot behind some old furniture where he pulled out the clothes he took from the hotel room and hid them behind the furniture. He knew he'd need them. He exited the building and looked for a pay phone. He dialed Rupert's without even thinking if that was the right thing to do, but he needed to find out why Rupert went to the hotel looking for him. Maybe he had news about the mission in Pakistan, or maybe something was going to take place in the building. The phone rang for a while, but no response. George hung up, waited couple of minutes, and dialed again.

"Hello!" Rupert answered after three rings.

"This is George! You were at the hotel looking for me, I heard. What's going on?"

"Need to talk," Rupert said.

"Talk about what? Listen, I think it's better if we don't cross paths, for now at least," George said.

"Sure! Suit yourself!" Rupert responded in a sarcastic tone. "Deal with ISI on your own when they find you. Goodbye," Rupert said, hanging the phone.

George turned Rupert's statement in his head and wondered what he meant by it. He stuck some coins in the pay phone and called him again.

"Hello, look we're done!" Rupert shouted.

"Wait, wait, wait! What did you mean by dealing with ISI on my own?" George insistently asked.

"Go ask them yourself if you want to know," Rupert said with an arrogant attitude.

"Look! Don't give me this garbage; I need to know what is going on. I have been chased by three people in a car and I have no idea what is going on here or what the ISI wants, so cut the B.S. and tell me what is happening," George explained, fuming.

"Okay, meet me at the usual place," Rupert suggested.

"When?" George asked.

"In an hour," Rupert said.

"I'll be there," George replied.

"If you're not there in an hour, I am gone," Rupert warned.

"I'll be there, I said." George hung up the phone tensely.

George made his way back to the empty building but didn't go in. He stood across the street, making sure Rupert was alone. Close to a half hour later, Rupert showed up, walking towards the building entrance alone. He went in. George saw him and followed. They met upstairs and without any greeting George said, "What is going on?"

"You need to find a way out," Rupert replied.

"What do you mean, a way out?" George questioned.

"The ISI want to arrest you really badly, and they are looking for anything they can dig up on you. So, you need to decide fast," Rupert explained.

"And how do you know all this?" George asked.

"Let's just say I know," Rupert responded.

With a panicked look on his face, George stood silent for few minutes thinking of a plan. All kinds of ideas went through his mind.

"I have to go," Rupert announced. "There has been much CIA activity in the building lately, and I don't want anyone to come in here and find us."

That explains the paper cups on the table, George thought.

"Look, here is a personal phone number. Don't call me unless absolutely necessary," Rupert offered George.

George took the number without saying anything.

Rupert was gone.

George stood there thinking what to do when he heard loud gun shots coming from outside. He ran out to find people running in every direction. Some gathered blocking the way to the main street. He pushed his way through the crowd, and suddenly there he was lying on the ground in a pool of blood. Rupert was shot.

George yelled, "Call an ambulance!" He pulled Rupert up, leaning him against the wall. People just stood there looking at Rupert in pain and George trying to stop the blood using part of Rupert's shirt he tore off. The wounds were too severe. George asked. "Who shot you?"

"I don't know…" Rupert replied, gasping for air. "Someone walked up to me, pulled out his gun, and just shot."

"Okay, just stay still. We need to get out of here," George offered.

Rupert grabbed George's arm. "You need to get out of here. I will be okay. The ISI wanted me to set you up so they can arrest you. I don't think the ISI is behind the shooting. They needed me to get to you. You need to leave this place. Remember when I said some CIA agents are not good communicators? You need to be careful who you talk to. The CIA protocol is known. Don't leave any trace. Agents are as good as operations; they all must end to exist."

Rupert knew more about the CIA's illegal operations in several countries than George realized. He talked to him about some CIA agents, especially Philip Lawson and Scott Conwell and their involvement in the blood diamond business in Kenya. That was where Rupert had been before he was sent to Pakistan. Both Philip and Scott knew about Rupert's past and that he would never refuse to eliminate somebody for money. He killed several agents in Kenya and other African countries. Two years after that he was transferred to Pakistan—not for any operation, but because Scott and Philip knew he spoke Urdu, and they figured sending him to Pakistan would make it easier to get rid of him and ultimately eliminate him.

Rupert closed his eyes, squeezing George's hand. "Listen," he said, barely able to speak. "Go to the building, and inside of one of the table legs, you'll find a small, velvet jewelry bag with a flash drive in it and also some diamonds. I stole them in Kenya while making a delivery to one of Scott's high connections, a government official in the Middle East, I didn't know exactly where. Nobody ever suspected the missing diamonds. I had no problem smuggling them into Pakistan. The flash drive has everything you must know about Scott, Philip, and others. Those diamonds were my way out of the CIA into a different life style in the Caribbean. I always wanted to live there. Now you can do whatever you want with the flash drive and the diamonds.

"Oh, one more thing, if you need any help, go find Masud and give him this password: "The paper street." He will know what that means. He has a shop in the market. Just ask for Masud and tell him, 'I am a friend of Rupert.'"

Paper Street was tucked in the back of the market, and the only way to get to it was through a back alley adjacent to the market coffee shop and a sandwich shop. The street was known for its black market and illegal money exchange. Millions in all currencies changed hands daily.

George tried to keep Rupert breathing, but it was too late. He died from his wounds. As George was leaving the scene, he got pulled aside and arrested for murder by the Pakistani police. They threw him in a car and sped away. He was jailed, and what made it worse for him was the gun in his possession. The gun was enough for the police to convict him of murder without comparing bullets with those that killed Rupert.

He was put in a maximum security cell with no windows or any contact with other prisoners. He spent two months in the cell. The only time the door opened was to hand him food or to interrogate him about Rupert's death.

After two months of detention, he was transferred to another cell with another inmate. George's new companion was quiet and just looked at him with an unusual interest. The guards pushed him in without saying anything. George felt like prey being pushed to the monster's mouth. He sat on his metal bed, and not a word passed between either of them.

George's cell mate, a Pakistani by origin with a somewhat heavy build, clean shaven with short hair, was busy looking through a magazine. For two days they didn't speak a word to one another. Each stayed in his space with a feeling of mistrust and suspicion.

Towards the end of the first week in the cell, the act that would change George's life forever took place. In the middle of the night, while George pretended to be a sleep, he saw his cellmate coming towards him with a pillow to strangle him. George, without hesitating, jumped out of the bed, and with his arms open, dove into the man's waist, dropping him back on to his bed.

They fought savagely. The man was heavier than George, so he easily pinned him against the wall and started punching him. In a move to free himself, George glanced over to a shelf next to him and grabbed a metal mug with a handle similar to the ones the military uses. Holding the mug by the handle, he swung it to the man's face with such force that it bent.

The aggressor slowed for a minute from the shock. That's when George head-butted him right in the middle of the face. Losing balance, the man held on to the wall, and George head-butted him again, and he fell on his knees. George tore a couple of pages from the magazine his opponent was reading and shoved them in his mouth as far as he could. Then he locked his arm around his neck as forcefully as he could, in an attempt to cut any air circulation. The man fought with two hands, but

George's anger and fear gave him a strength that he had never shown. He kept holding to the man's neck until he was sure that he was dead.

When the ordeal was over, George pulled the papers out the dead man's mouth, pulled him onto his bed, and then crawled back on his own. The prison guards knew what was going on but never showed up to check. They had been instructed to leave it alone.

George's cellmate was a CIA agent who had been arrested in Pakistan at the request of Philip Lawson, and through one of his highly-placed government officials in Pakistan, held for defamation of the Agency and suspicion of treason. He was awaiting extradition back to the U.S. to stand trial. That never happened.

Early the next morning some guards showed up to the cell. George was already up, and the other was still lying in bed. The guards yelled "Get up!" but he did not answer. One of them unlocked the door and walked in, poking the guy on the shoulder with his wooden baton. No response. He turned around looked at George and said to the other guard, "He is dead!"

The second guard rushed in to check if he was really dead. "You killed him!" he shouted at George.

"No, I was asleep. I have no idea what happened!" George defended himself.

"You killed him," the guard insisted.

"I am telling you, I have no idea what happened to him!" George continued.

The two guards pushed George against the wall and handcuffed him. "Turn around; sit down," one of them ordered. George sat on the edge of the bed trying to keep calm.

"How did you kill him?" one of the guards asked.

"I didn't kill him. I was asleep all night, and I have no idea what you are talking about," George said, raising his voice, thinking maybe some intimidation would get them both off his back.

Soon, the director of the prison showed up with two more guards. "Why did you kill him?" the director asked George, slapping him across the face.

George made a move to stand up, but the guards pushed him back down. "I didn't kill him, I said!" George replied with angry voice.

"Throw him in solitary," the director ordered. "A week should give him something to think about," he continued on his way out.

George was led to a dark, underground room reserved only for notorious criminals. The room had a cement floor, with water dripping from a special system hanging in the ceiling to keep the floor wet and freezing cold at all times. George sat in the corner of the dark room, contemplating what might come next. During that time he thought about Isabella and Silvia.

While George was living through these horrific times, Isabella decided to move back to Lebanon. There was not much for her to do in the U.S., and she wanted to be where Albert was. Silvia, on the other hand, was still working in her job, and not much had changed.

George spent a whole week in that room. He would get food, but that was it. Nothing else. After a week in solitary, he was interrogated by the cops again as to what happened that night in the cell.

He gave them the same answer. "I don't know what happened to him."

They locked him again in a cell and literarily threw the key away.

Escaping crossed his mind many times, but how? He had no chance of ever making it out of the cell. He was now a criminal waiting for whatever they decide to do with him. Ten days later, after being tortured and interrogated time and again, George was unexpectedly let go. Skip had not heard from George for a while, so he phoned Philip to ask him if he had heard from George, but Philip said no. Worried that Skip might somehow find out what happened, Philip made a call to the Pakistanis

"Get him out of there, but make sure he doesn't leave Pakistan alive," Philip said to his Pakistani contact.

George was freed but not safe. Without any questions asked, they let him go but warned him that he would be back. George could not comprehend what just happened. He thought,

"Maybe they caught Rupert's assassin, or maybe this was a plan to get him killed." He left anyway.

His first stop was the building. He went straight to the table where he first saw those empty paper cups. He flipped it upside down and unscrewed all four legs.

There it was, just as Rupert said: a velvet jewelry bag wrapped with a golden string so it fit in the small table leg opening. He pulled it out, opened it, and took the flash drive and the sparkling handful of diamonds. He then changed to different clothes—the ones he had hidden behind the furniture—and left in a hurry.

George wanted to get out of town to someplace safe. He walked briskly with his head tucked between his shoulders so that he would not be recognized. He crossed through an alley and got out on another side, not too far from a plaza where long-distance buses parked. He purchased a bus ticket for Ramli and stood in a corner, giving his back to the wall. The time was now 3:45 p.m., and the place was getting crowded with people waiting for buses heading in different directions. It was not until 4:25 that his ride showed up, packed with people. It took another 15 minutes or so to get everybody off.

Finally, the bus headed to Ramli, and George felt more relaxed once he was out of town safely. He was the richest man on the bus, and he thought for a second about pulling the bag out for a second look. He stuck his hand in his pocket but hesitated. He didn't want to attract any attention.

The situation in the safe house was not the same as he had left it. It was trashed when he walked in; someone had visited the house, and whoever came in was obviously looking for something that was in the house. Things were spread all over the floor, but nothing was missing. He had rummaged through some things he had hidden in the house, pulled a phone card, and left the house looking for a pay phone. The closest one was in a business strip mall which also had a teashop, a clothing store, an herbal shop, and a pharmacy.

"Assalam Alaikum," he said.

"*Wa- Alaikum Asslam*," the owner behind his small counter replied.

"I need to use the phone," George asked.

The proprietor directed him to a cabin. "Here we go," George thought. He didn't care what time it was. He pulled the card out and proceeded dialing Skip's cell phone number.

"Skip speaking," a voice sounded tired on the other end.

"George here!"

"How are you doing?" Skip asked.

"What is going on here?" George replied. "It's been a living hell."

"Calm down, George, and tell me what's been happening," Skip calmly asked.

"Who's involved here from the Agency? Is anybody working with the ISI?" George asked.

"Yeah, all of us are. Pakistan is one of the U.S. government's main concerns," Skip explained.

"Do you know someone with the name Rupert De Paz?" George asked.

"I heard this name somewhere. Why?" Skip said.

"Do you know he is dead? He was shot," George told Skip. "What do you know about Philip Lawson and Scott Conwell?" George asked, further surprising Skip.

"Not much, beside their work and what they do," Skip said. "Why?"

"Do you know anything about operation 'Stone' in Africa?" George asked. That was the last thing Rupert told George before he died.

"Yeah, that was a case of diamond trafficking in Africa and Europe." Skip replied. "Where are you now?" Skip asked.

"I am still in Pakistan?" George replied.

"Where in Pakistan?" Skip asked.

"I have to run, I'll call you later," George said in a hurry, refusing to answer Skip's question.

Now George was more confused than ever before, his mind racing, refusing to think that Skip was involved somehow. He said thank you to the shop keeper and walked out. After talking to Skip, neither the safe house nor any other place in Pakistan was safe for George. He made the decision to leave Pakistan before anything happened. The closest country was Afghanistan, but Afghanistan was not any safer than Pakistan.

George made his final plan to leave but was worried about being caught with the diamonds and the flash drive. Eyes were everywhere. He decided to do it anyway.

Two days later he called Skip back, asking him to get him out of Pakistan. Skip couldn't do much. He told him the mission was not finished yet, and that he couldn't just make the decision to get him out. George listened to Skip's words, while at the same time thinking about a way to get out.

Skip said, "We can't just leave the place to the Russians. Russian Intelligence agents are all over Pakistan, and we need to know what Russia's plan is in the region.

George argued with Skip for few minutes, trying to convince him to get him out, but Skip insisted that it was beyond his power. The call did not end the way George was hoping, and that was the last time they spoke.

Some days after that phone call George was in Afghanistan. He paid a merchant $200.00 to help him cross the border on a donkey, away from the customs. Afghan merchants knew all the back roads and hidden pathways between Pakistan and Afghanistan. They cross to get supplies and don't like to pay custom duties for their wares, so they avoid the legal crossings.

Afghanistan was not any better than Pakistan, as George had a strange feeling that he was not alone, that someone knew his whereabouts. Afghanistan had become a place where one could not distinguish who is who. The country was full of secret agents from different countries, terrorists, and drug dealers. The danger for George was all around. He feared he would never leave Afghanistan, not even Kabul; he spent much of his time hiding in places that were not often frequented. At this point, he doubted anyone he came in contact with— even the landlord from whom he rented a room in a small house.

Scott and Philip had long-reaching hands, and they could hit anywhere they wanted. They knew George had fled Pakistan, and it only made sense to them that the closest crossing was to Afghanistan. Somehow, they managed to put George's name on a black list of people dealing in opium, selling it to drug cartels in various countries. Philip contacted the police chief in Kabul and told him George's story, but the chief didn't buy it, because he knew that the opium business was not for everyone. The elite group controlling this business would never allow an outsider to come to Afghanistan to learn the secret of the trade. However, as a routine operation and to show that the government in Afghanistan was not corrupt, the authorities, with only a description and a photo sent by Philip, decided to find George and question him. But he was never found.

George's last conversation on the phone with Skip made him explore every option possible to get out of the lion's mouth as far and as quickly as possible. When Skip mentioned the Russian Intelligence, George thought about going to Russia, but knew that he would be traced from his plane ticket. He purchased two tickets, one back to the U.S and another one to Russia; neither of those tickets were ever used. George crossed back to

Pakistan in hope that Scott and Philip would think that he used one of those tickets.

Even though in Pakistan, the name George Munssif had disappeared from Philip's radar, he was still worried about being recognized. He stayed very close to places he was familiar with, trying to find a way to leave the country without attracting any unwanted attention. For days George tried to think of how he would escape Pakistan, but had no clear path to follow. His U.S. passport and his name would eventually be recognized at any airport. With all the confusion and fear, George's only alternative was to buy or steal any documents that could give him a way out. He remembered Rupert saying, "Go see Masud if you need help." George made his way to the market, hoping that Masud was the right guy for the job.

He asked the first person he encountered in the market, "Where can I find Masud?"

"Who is Masud?" The stranger replied.

"He has a shop here in the market," George explained.

"What kind of shop?" The stranger further asked.

"I don't know," George said, somewhat nervous.

"Come, come, follow me," the stranger suggested.

George, hesitated for a minute, then followed the stranger.

"Do you know Masud?" the stranger asked a shop keeper.

"Is it Masud International?" the shop keeper asked. "That is the only Masud I know in the market."

"The stranger turned around looking at George, "Is it international?"

George said, "I just know Masud."

"Okay, come on," the stranger replied.

They both walked a few hundred feet to a shop filled with exotic items from around the world, while George looked everywhere to make sure they were not followed. The stranger started shouting, "Masud, Masud, Masud," from outside the shop.

"Coming!" a voice replied. "Yes?" the short man said after shaking hands with George's new companion.

"This man is looking for Masud and I don't know if it's you or another Masud."

"Hello, sir. Can you help me? Do you know Rupert?" George asked.

"Who?" Masud replied.

"Rupert," George repeated.

"No, never heard this name," Masud said.

"He told me go see Masud in the market," George insisted.

"No, I don't know this person!" Masud was getting agitated, walking back inside the store.

"Wait, wait, wait! 'Paper Street.'"

Masud suddenly froze, then took few steps back towards George. "What do you know about 'Paper Street'?" he asked

"Nothing. Rupert said to tell you 'Paper Street' before he died," George replied.

"Come in, come in." Masud rushed George inside. "Don't let anyone hear you saying this around here," he muttered. "I know Rupert is dead and that for me is the past. What do you need?"

"I need papers to get out of Pakistan," George said.

"What papers?" Masud asked.

"Passport," George answered.

"I don't do passports," Masud refused, shaking his head.

"I'll pay you anything you want," George offered.

"No, that is very dangerous," Masud responded.

"Look, my life is in danger and I need to leave the country," George said, trying to convince Masud.

"This is big and not cheap. Let me think about it," Masud said, cockily. "Where can I contact you? Don't come to the shop anymore. There are eyes everywhere."

"I have no place. Can I swing by in couple of days?" George asked.

"Not here. Go to 'Paper Street' and wait by the fountain at 10 a.m. I'll find you," Masud said. "Leave now," he ordered.

George rushed away without saying a word. He spent the next days hiding in the building where he and Rupert met. During the second night he heard a conversation going on between two people.

"The Silver Head wants to find George Munssif as soon as possible," one of them said. "Silver Head" was a code name for Philip because of his grey hair.

"He wants him out of the picture once for all. Rupert is no risk anymore," he continued.

"Where is he?" the other one asked.

"I don't know. He might be hiding in Afghanistan," the first replied. "We need to find him before something happens," he added.

"Are we going to Afghanistan?" the second voice asked.

"Not before we get the order from the Silver Head," was the response.

George could not see the two people in the dark. He kept quiet and listened. A few minutes later, a phone rang.

"Hello!" one of the two people answered. "Yes sir, I understand, we'll get on it right away." The call ended.

"We're going to Afghanistan; the subject was in Afghanistan few days ago. That was Silver Head."

George was relieved to hear that Afghanistan was the point of focus for his search. The next morning, he left for Paper Street to meet Masud. He waited by the fountain as instructed. An hour later and close to 11:05, he had seen no sign of Masud. He started getting worried that something had happened to him. He waited until 11:30 before he decided to leave. A young man accosted him on the way out. "Masud is waiting for you." The young man said. "Follow me!"

George followed him to the back of a store where Masud was waiting inside. "I thought you said 10:00 by the fountain," George said in an unhappy tone.

"I don't know who you are and can't just trust somebody I meet for the first time," Masud explained. "Now, tell me, how do you know Rupert?" Masud needed to be reassured.

"It's a long story," George said.

"Tell me anyway," Masud insisted.

"We were business partners. We knew each other back from the US, and Rupert had some problems with some business people here. I don't know what kind of problems. He never told me. And I don't know why he was killed." George tried to keep the story as real as he could. "And now some people are after me. I don't even know what they want. They tried to arrest me and even kill me."

Masud listened attentively. "What kind of business you were in with Rupert?" Masud interrogated.

"We traveled different places buying merchandise to take back to the States," George said.

"Hmmm..." Masud made a skeptical noise. "Has Rupert ever been involved in any shady business deals?" he asked.

"I don't know. He never told me anything."

"He was very involved in the Opium business," Masud told George. "Anyway, I can get you papers, but you have to pay $600.00 U.S. dollars," Masud offered.

"When can I get them?" George replied without hesitation.

"Give me two days. Do you have pictures?" Masud asked.

George pulled two passport pictures out of his pocket and handed them to Masud.

"Advance!" Masud requested. "Half now and half when you get the papers."

George search in his pockets and found $250.00 US dollars. "Here," he extended his hand.

"I said half. This is only $250.00 U.S. dollars," Masud protested, handing the money back to George.

"That's all I have now. I will get you the rest when I pick up the passport." He convinced Masud that he had no more money.

"Okay," Masud said. "No money in full, no passport."

"No problem," George agreed.

"Come back in three days," Masud said.

George left, wondering where he was going to find the remaining money to pay Masud. Walking through the Paper Market, he looked at people secretly handing each other money, exchanging different currencies. He even saw jewelry being sold, shining from a distance, moving from one hand to another. He thought about selling a couple of diamonds, but decided not to.

He was worried it would open up a whole new chapter of problems he was not willing to deal with.

He made his way through the market into the main street, when he was surprised to see a couple of white men heading toward him. He immediately suspected them. He turned around and lost himself in the crowded, open air market. George knew that the two men were not tourists; CIA agents are trained to sense danger. George bumped into a couple of people as he rushed to exit the market from the back side, saying "Sorry" in Urdu.

He stopped around the corner from the market to make sure he wasn't followed. He didn't see anyone. He knew at that moment that Pakistan was as dangerous as Afghanistan. It was not the time for him to chance being seen. He lived in constant fear that he would never make it out of Pakistan. Now, Silver Head was all over the place, and he knew what was at stake, as his entire career and life depended on George's arrest or even assassination.

Three days later, George, as agreed, showed up at Masud's hidden store in the back of the Paper Market after waiting again by the fountain for the young man to come escort him. George knew the routine and didn't mind it. Masud was afraid for his life and wanted to be sure that no one was watching.

George walked into the store with the young man. "Masud!" he yelled walking in.

Masud peeked from behind a curtain and said "Thank you" to the young man. "You can go now," he politely requested.

Masud then waved to George, "Come here." He took him in the back of the store. "Do you have the money?" He quickly asked.

"Where are the papers?" George announced.

Masud pulled out a Pakistani passport and handed it to George. "This is real. It's not fake," he said.

George opened the passport to check it out. His name was Faycal Khawaja.

"What do you think?" Masud proudly asked.

"Good!" George replied.

"One thing," Masud told George. "It's better if you do not use the passport in a Pakistani airport. I prefer that you go to another country and use it there. Just to be safe."

"Can I use it from Afghanistan?" George asked, testing Masud.

"If you want," Masud said. "Now, the money."

"I do not have the money, but I have something expensive that you will like," George said, trying to get Masud's attention.

Masud grabbed the passport from George's hand with force and anger. "Meeting is over. Please leave."

"Wait a minute!" George insisted. He unclasped his Royal Oak watch and handed it to Masud. "Here, this is a very expensive watch. You can sell it and take the money," George enthusiastically offered.

"No, no," Masud replied. "I need the money."

"This is a more than $800.00 U.S. dollars watch," George argued.

Masud took the watch, examining it very closely. "Why don't you sell it and bring the money?" Masud said.

"You know the market better than I do, and you can sell it," George said.

After few minutes thinking about George's offer, Masud pronounced, "I will keep the watch and the passport. If the watch sells I will give you the passport, and if not, you can have your watch back."

George had to agree to the deal. "Okay," he replied.

The watch had great sentimental value for George, because it was Isabella's gift to him after graduating college. She even had his initials (G.M.) engraved in the band.

"Come back in few days," Masud ordered.

"When?" George asked.

"It's going to take time to sell the watch," Masud replied. "In a week."

"A week is too long; I need to get out of here!" George protested.

"Three days," Masud said.

To make time pass, George spent the next three days planning his exit out of Pakistan. He needed to have all details in place. Going to Afghanistan was now a suicide mission for George, since he heard the conversation of the two people in the building. Using a passport in a Pakistani airport could be trouble as well.

After the agreed-upon three days had passed, Masud waited impatiently for George. He had to get rid of the passport, not because he was afraid, but because money was a priority for him. George followed the previous instructions, standing by the fountain. Masud looked at George, gesturing with his head to follow him to the back.

"I couldn't sell your watch for more than $200.00 U.S. dollars," Masud said.

"This is an $800.00 watch," George replied, his annoyance evident.

Masud knew the real value of the watch, but wanted to push for more. "Sorry," he sarcastically said. "Give me $200 dollars more with the watch," he demanded.

"I don't have any money," George replied with a desperate look on his face.

After several minutes of negotiations, Masud handed the passport to George. "Here, I don't do this with anybody. But, this time it's okay."

It wasn't true; Masud had done this many times before. He would turn around and sell the watch for more than a thousand dollars on Paper Street. He knew how things were done.

George left in hurry before Masud had a chance to say anything else. He was prepared to take a chance with the fake Pakistani passport. At the bus station everything seemed normal: hundreds of people waiting for buses. George could easily be lost in the crowd with nobody noticing him. Making his way to the ticket booth, he approached the open counter.

"Hello, when is the next bus to Durand Line?" George asked.

"At 12:45 p.m.," the clerk replied, looking at the bus schedule.

"One ticket, please," George requested. "How much?"

"3640.00 Rupees," the clerk said. ($40.00 U.S. dollars).

George pulled out a $50.00 bill and asked "Can I pay with this?"

"Yes, but I give you the change in Rupees, Okay?"

"No problem," George replied.

Handing him the ticket and the change in Rupees, the clerk asked George for an ID so he could write the name on the passengers list. "All passengers have to be registered for security reasons," the clerk explained after George asked why.

George pulled his new Pakistani passport and hand it to the clerk.

"Are you from Pakistan?" the clerk asked. "You speak perfect English," he added.

"Oh, thank you! My parents are from here. I was born and raised in the U.S.," George replied, smiling.

"America! I hear it's a beautiful country, but I don't like the government," the clerk commented.

"Yes, it's a beautiful country," George said, leaving out the clerk's comment about the government.

"You're going to Afghanistan for vacation?" the clerk asked in a curious tone.

"I have a friend who lives right on the border whom I haven't seen in years; I am going to visit him." George carefully picked his answers.

"Oh, okay. The drive is very nice, but long," the clerk said.

"Thank you!" George said, leaving the counter.

As usual, the bus was an hour late, and George was on his way out of Pakistan. During the one and a half day bus ride with frequent stops, George looked at everyone who got on or off the bus. He never slept, though he would from time to time lean his head back against the worn out and partially torn head rest and close his eyes; but he never really fell asleep. With every stop the bus made, George would look at everyone coming and going.

Although he was armed and ready for any unexpected event, he was no match for Philip. Philip could strike anywhere and anytime. He had done it before with other agents who got in his way. Rupert was one of them. George's only worry was how to get the flash drive and the diamonds to a safe place. He could not trust anyone, not even Skip. Everybody around him was a potential threat. Silvia was the last confidant he could think of.

He needed someone's help and felt Silvia was the only person he could trust.

Finally, the Afghan border was within meters, and George could see the armed men standing and waiting for the bus to pull up. The passengers lined up in front of the custom agents, handing out their permits and passports one by one. When George's turn came, he had his passport already in hand, and passed it to the customs agent with a smile. The agent took it and spoke to George in Pashtun.

"Why are you coming to Afghanistan?"

"For a visit," George replied in Pashto.

"Have you been to Afghanistan before?" the agent continued.

"No, this is the first time," George replied.

"Do you know anyone in Afghanistan?" the agent questioned.

"No," George said.

"How long are you staying?" the agent asked.

"A few days or a week," George carefully announced.

"What is the purpose of your visit?" The agent kept fishing for information.

"I heard great things about your country and came to visit."

George was shaking inside from fear that the agent would ask more questions about the passport and any other documents proving he was Pakistani. Luckily, the custom agent didn't go that far. After turning the pages of the passport back and forth while looking at George, he stamped the first page and handed George the passport back. "Welcome," he said.

George was now free in Afghanistan and at least out of Pakistan.

Not very far from the city center in Kabul, George found a small house that the owner converted to a guest house, renting the three rooms for some extra cash. It had a hand-written "For Rent" sign. It was affordable and would not attract any unwanted attention until he figured out his next move. He spent a few nights at the house, staying away from Kabul.

The only connection George had with the outside world was to walk to the store across the street and back. Everything had a price in Afghanistan, and people were willing to do anything for an extra buck. The smuggling of contraband, both merchandise and people, in and out of the country was a daily activity that many Afghans practiced as a business. Money really talked in Afghanistan, and George almost run out of it, except for a few dollars. He was left with only one option: to sell one of the diamonds he had.

Not knowing where to start, he made his way to the city to find a place. His first attempt was the bazaars lining the narrow strip of the market entrance. These bazaars are familiar with foreigners exchanging currency, so George felt that this might be a good place to start shopping for a buyer. After talking to few dealers and not agreeing on a price, he walked in to a small shop selling East Asian decoration items imported from the Far East. The man was arranging some of the goods he just received when George pronounced "*Assalam Alaikum.*"

The man replied, "*Wa-Alaikum Assalam.*"

George browsed the store, looking at different items. He was careful in his plan to approach the shopkeeper. He asked a few questions in Pashto about the items he was looking at, and the shopkeeper was happy answering every question George asked. A few minutes went by with the two still talking when George asked, "I am trying to sell a diamond that I have had for some time, and don't know where to find a buyer."

"Can I see it?" the shopkeeper asked.

George pulled the small diamond from underneath his long Afghani shirt and carefully handed it to the shopkeeper.

The man examined the diamond closely and said, "How much does it weigh?"

"I don't know," George replied.

"How much you want for it?" the man asked.

"What do you think it is worth?" George asked. He had a price in mind but wanted the shopkeeper to make an offer.

The man walked behind his wooden counter, pulled out a small scale, and gently set the diamond on it. "One-half carat," he said after adjusting his scale several times, making sure that it worked properly.

"You can get 25,000.00 Afghani." This was a little under $500.00. The shop keeper knew that was not the real value, but was testing George to see how desperate he was for money.

George said, smiling, "That is much less than the value of the diamond," extending his hand asking for the gem.

But the man wasn't going to let George get off that easily with such a precious piece. He insisted, "The most you will get for it is 30, 000.00 Afghani." (About $650.00.)

George was still hoping the shop keeper would not give up and offer more for the diamond. After going back and forth for some time, the deal was done and George let the diamond go for $795.00 (41,567.00 Afghani). George's mission with that money was clear. First, he kept some to pay his overdue rent; second, some to pay his way out of Afghanistan; and with the rest, he went straight to looking for a place to call Silvia. Her phone rang late in evening in the US.

She first saw *No Caller ID* displayed on her cell phone screen. "These stupid marketers, they even call cell phones now," she muttered to herself.

But George kept trying. It wasn't until the fifth time when she answered the phone.

"Hello!" she said in a settled and yet annoyed voice.

"Hello, is this Silvia?" George replied in a fearful way, thinking maybe it was someone else.

"Who's speaking?" Silvia asked, curious who it might be.

"This is George," he said.

"George who?" she asked, still wondering who it was.

"George Munssif," he replied, hesitating a little.

"George! Really, is that you? Where are you calling from?" Silvia's face shined in the asking.

"Yes, it's me. Afghanistan. I need to talk to you."

"Afghanistan! Go ahead," she enthusiastically pronounced.

"Listen, I need your help," George said.

"What kind of help?" Silvia replied.

"I have some stuff that I must get to you, and no one should know about what I am about to tell you. I mean no one." George wanted to make sure Silvia understood the importance.

"What stuff?" She wondered.

"I have a flash drive and some diamonds that must make it to the U.S." George explained.

"What flash drive and diamonds?" Silvia sounded confused.

"Is your line secure?" George asked, making sure that her cell phone was not bugged.

"Yes, what is going on?" Silvia interrupted him.

"Do the names Scott Conwell and Philip Lawson mean anything to you?" George asked.

Silvia paused for a second before saying, "I've heard those names before."

"The flash drive is a list of some tainted names dealing in illegal business in Kenya and other parts of Africa. The diamonds are proof of that," George explained.

"Where did you get this information?" Silvia pressed.

"Can't go into details now," George said. "I need to get out of Afghanistan. Scott and Philip are everywhere and I am sure they will find me soon if I don't get out of here."

Silvia listened as George spoke.

"I need to go now," George suddenly said. "I'll call again."

He made his way out of the phone booth inside the store, heading towards a busy open space market. He began his plan to get out of Afghanistan as soon as he could.

The open space market, or *souk* as it's known in Afghanistan, was hustling and bustling with people. Vegetables stands, clothing stores, all had goods lying along the curbside, sitting on plastic tarps so they did not get wet or dirty. Dealers of smuggled gold, silver and even diamonds stood there, waiting for those interested in buying the expensive wares to approach them. These dealers had everything tucked in their pockets, and sometimes they worked with store owners, leaving their merchandise with them for a cut of the sale price. They did that so they would not be noticed by the local police, who sometimes raid the market for illegal activities. George learned a few tricks from being in Pakistan, especially from Rupert. One of those tricks was the ability to size up people and situations and to know how to sweet talk people into giving up information.

He approached one of those dealers and asked in Pashto, "Do you know Masud the diamond dealer?" Masud was the name of the store owner in Pakistan who got George the passport.

"Masud who?" the stranger replied.

"A short guy. A fast-talker who sits here all the time buying and selling diamonds," George said.

"No, I don't know him," the stranger replied.

George put his hand in his pocket and pulled out a stack of money, brandishing it in front of the guy. "Sorry, I must have made a mistake; I need him for some business," George improvised.

"What business?" the man asked, staring at the stack of money.

"Never mind. I'll find him," George said.

"Maybe I can help," the man replied. "What business? Do you have gold, silver, or something expensive to sell?" the man asked.

"No, but I need to cross the border to Uzbekistan to bring some expensive merchandise." George now waited for the man's reaction.

"Uzbekistan!" the stranger said, surprised.

"Yes, Uzbekistan," George said.

"Why not by plane?" the man asked.

"I can't bring it with me if I travel by plane," George replied. "I need to cross by land."

"It's far away, days on the road and crossing mountains. Not safe," the man commented.

"I'll take my chances," George said.

"How much would you pay to cross?" The stranger was showing signs of interest after seeing the money.

"How much do you charge?" George played it tough.

In a very diplomatic way, the stranger said, "For you, only 35,000 Afghani." ($700.00)

"That's too much. How about 25,000 Afghani?" George said.

"No, no, it's too difficult for that little money," the man replied. "Okay, 30,000 Afghani," he continued after a pause.

"I can't do that; all I have is 25,000 Afghani," George insisted.

"Sorry, not enough," the man said.

George put the money back in his pocket and started walking away.

"Wait, wait! For 25,000 Afghani I will take you halfway, and you continue. Is that a deal?" The man wanted that money.

George thought for a second and said, "How far?"

"Not very far from the border," the man replied.

George agreed and they shook hands. They made arrangements to meet the next day late in the evening to start their journey.

They both met the next day at 7:45 p.m. by a rusty, abandoned watershed that once housed the main water supply for the city, but was now empty. The local officials had plans to get it out and use the space for something else but never did. The money kept disappearing.

As Afghan merchants are used to carrying supplies on mules, the stranger showed up hauling enough trip supplies on the back of a mule to last the duration of the 2-3 day's walk. George knew how Afghanis travel because he had seen it before, and for that reason, he did not comment. He followed behind the man, walking at a modest pace heading south out of town.

That night the temperature was low, and the cool air coming from the mountains gave a feeling of even harsher weather closer to the border. George was armed, and so was the guide, with a curved sword which handle engraved with a historical design from a centuries-old Afghani dynasty. He had it tucked under the piece of cloth covering the back of the mule.

That particular road was known to have thugs and opium dealers surfacing out of nowhere, trapping merchants for their cash and supplies. Fortunately for the two, they crossed several other traders, some going in their direction and others coming back.

Almost four days later, and after crossing mountains, remote valleys, and villages, walking in the dark trying to avoid deadly cliffs, they arrived in the early evening to a crossing where they could see the border from afar.

"We have arrived," the stranger suddenly said to George. "I must return. You can see the border from here."

George looked a little scared to be left alone to try to figure out how to finish the rest of the journey. Although the journey so far had been long and tiring, the man made it seem less daunting.

After giving him the rest of the money, George said "Thank you" and started walking away. The man stopped for a minute counting the money, then arranging his belongings on the mule, took a drink of water, and went on his way. A few feet away, he turned and yelled at George, "Wait!"

George turned around. The man let loose his mule and walked to George. "You will need this," he said and gave him a piece of paper with a prayer written on it. "This has helped me many times. Take it," the man offered.

"Thank you!" George replied, folding the paper, placing it in the palm of his right hand, and firmly closing his hand. He had another few hours to walk before reaching the border.

At dawn, George made his way through a wooded area on the north side of the border where he could see custom agents standing, smoking cigarettes, and chatting. The post was an old barrack with some roof shingles torn and some missing. The metal barrier, about 15 feet long, was bolted to a rusty anchor blocking the entrance. Each time a car came by, one of the agents jumped up to manually open it.

George walked calmly, then positioned himself on the ground to crawl and not be noticed. One of the agents put out his cigarette and walked towards the wooded area. George froze, thinking that he saw him. He pulled his gun and quietly held it, aiming at the agent. A few feet from where George was hiding, the agent stopped, stood there for a while, coughed couple of times, and started urinating. George kept an eye on him the whole time with his gun pointing at the agent, ready to pull the trigger.

"*Amir*!" the other guard yelled.

"*Ha*!" Amir replied.

"*Telefon*," the guard said.

"*Allo, Salom*!" Amir pronounced, grabbing the handset sitting on the table. It was his wife, checking what time he would be home.

"Not until tomorrow morning," Amir replied.

That was George's only chance to get away. He got up and quickly ran through the woods. Half a mile down the road, he changed his clothes and ditched the Afghani ones over a nearby cliff. The road was empty, and only few trucks were making their way to the city. Some were full of deliveries, others were empty. He hitchhiked for about half an hour before a truck driver pulled to the side to pick him up. The driver knew a few Arabic words he had learned while living in the Gulf, but no English.

"*Salom*," George said.

"*Salom*," the driver replied.

"Going to the city?" George asked in Arabic.

"*Ha!*" The driver replied.

Striking a conversation with George in broken Arabic but mostly Uzbek, the driver asked George if he lived in the area. George had to find a quick answer.

"I live on the other side of town. Not too far." He then quickly changed the subject, asking the driver how many times he drove back and forth on this road.

"Two or three times, and sometimes four times a week, depending on the stuff to be delivered," the driver explained, still in broken Arabic.

About an hour later, the driver pulled to the city center of Tashkent, the capital. A feeling of ancient history permeated this beautiful city, and yet, it had a very western ambiance. With its modern architecture and vibrating life style, one could easily feel at home. Markets with their famous Asian spices, stands of fruits and vegetables, restaurants and bars, all made Tashkent a lively city.

George thanked the driver and hopped out of the big truck near the famous square. He did not know the square, but that was the closest place to everything in town. From there, he walked through the square trying to find a place for the night. Hotels of all kinds and prices were in Tashkent, from five stars to low budget. George settled for a hidden gem on Mirabad Street that he stumbled on by pure chance. At about $50 U.S. dollars a night, it sounded very good to George with the little money he had left from selling one of the diamonds back in Afghanistan. The small hotel was well taken care of, and the aroma of spices coming from the kitchen made it even more inviting.

"Hello," George said, walking toward the front desk.

"Hello," the young man replied.

"Do you have a room available?" George asked

"How many people?" The polite young man asked in a heavy English accent.

"Just one," George said.

The young man flipped some pages on his reservations note book. No computer in sight. Everything was written down by hand. He looked over some reservations and said, "Yes, I have one room left at 103,300 UZS."

"Can I can pay with Afghani? That's the only money I have," George asked.

"Just a minute!" The clerk said. He disappeared for a minute and came back. "Yes, you can."

"Good!" George said, smiling.

"How much that will be in Afghani?" he asked.

The clerk pulled out his small Sanyo calculator and punched in some numbers. "That will be 62,620 Afghani," he said.

George handed over enough money to pay for three nights.

The room was pleasantly arranged and clean, with a round corner table by the window and a neatly made bed with cotton of white sheets and pillow cases that smelled like rosemary.

Chapter 5
THE CLOSING CIRCLE

While George was roaming the world from one country to another fearing for his life, Silver Head's frustration was mounting. George was a loose cannon with the information he was holding against him. He even had a conflict with his main guy, Scott, on how to handle George's case. Silver Head wanted to track George wherever he was and get rid of him, while Scott had a different plan. His idea involved luring George back to the States and building a case of national treason and espionage for the Taliban against him, which would give him an automatic life sentence in prison. The two had major differences. Silver Head did not want to take such a risk, because Scott's plan could cause more problems. Scott did not want to kill George until he got those diamonds and the flash drive back. So they kept butting heads every time they talked about putting an end to George's life.

Skip Hallaway also wanted to know what had happened to George. He asked Silvia if she had any information, but she denied that he called her couple of times. George had not contacted Skip since he had last asked him to get him out Pakistan. George was not sure whether he should call him back or not, as he was doubting everyone around him. Silvia was hoping that George would call again so she can find out more from him. Sure enough, three days later, George called her cell phone late at night.

"Hi, Silvia. This is George."

"Hi. George," Silvia replied. "Where are you calling from?" she asked.

"Uzbekistan," he replied. "I need to get out of here and back to the US," George continued.

"You understand that you cannot just fly into the U.S.? Your name is everywhere. Even Skip asked about few days ago."

"Is Skip dirty too?" he asked.

"I don't know. He just asked if I knew where you were," Silvia said. "I think the safest way for you to travel now is to go to Canada. From there you can make your way to the U.S. by land," she suggested.

George listened to her, thinking that she was probably correct and that she would not turn him in. He did not say anything except, "I will call you again in few days when I have a plan. Thanks and bye!"

"George? Hello, George?" Silvia called twice. She wanted to tell him to be careful, but George was already gone.

George did not waste any time. He booked a flight to London the next day. He didn't have enough money to buy the ticket, and once again Isabella was there to help. He called her in Lebanon. She was shocked to hear from him after all that time.

"Hi, Mom. It's me, George. How are you?"

"George! How are you and where are you?"

"I am on a business trip and I need to buy a ticket from Uzbekistan to London and Canada. All my stuff, including my credit cards and papers, were stolen from my hotel room. Can you buy them for me? I will send you the money when I get home," George asked.

"Sure, not a problem. When do you want the tickets?" she asked.

"As soon as possible. Tomorrow if you can. I need to get home," George commented.

"Okay!" Isabella said.

"I'll call back in few hours to get the flight information from you. Thanks mom. Love you," George said before he hung up the phone.

Three hours later, George's trip was booked for the next day. He called back Isabella to confirm his itinerary and say thank you.

She asked him if she was going to see him sometime.

"I will schedule a trip to come out to see you when I get back to the U.S.," he told her.

The next morning, George went to Tashkent International Airport. The six-and-a-half hour flight was on time. He got to London with his U.S. passport, which did not require him to have a visa for the country. He waited at Heathrow Airport for few hours to board the plane for Montreal, Canada. Now in familiar territory, he felt at home; however, he was still not sure what would come next.

Almost week went by before he decided to call Silvia to let her know that he was in Canada. They both made a plan for him to travel to the closest U.S. border by bus, and she would be waiting for him right by the U.S. side of the border. George arrived to the customs at 6:45 p.m. on a Tuesday evening. Three customs agents boarded the luxurious bus, which was nothing like the buses George had been used to in Pakistan and Afghanistan. Two men and a woman were in dark uniforms with badges hanging on the front right pocket of their shirts clearly displaying "United States Government." Looking at those badges made George sick to his stomach, because it reminded him of Silver Head and Scott.

One by one, passengers were handing over their travel documents. Most had their visas, but a few were taken off the bus to be further interrogated. As for George, the lady officer said, "Hello, sir," after he handed her his U.S. passport.

"Hello," George replied.

"Do you live in Canada?" she asked.

"No, I live in the U.S.," George politely answered.

"Were you visiting Canada or on a business trip?" she continued.

"No, I flew to Canada yesterday from Asia," he explained.

"What do you do?" the agent asked.

"I am a buyer for a clothing company," he said.

"I'll be right back," the agent said, walking away with George's passport.

George was now contemplating the worst as he sat there waiting for the agent to come back. Almost 20 minutes went by before the agent showed up holding George's passport. "Thank you sir, have a safe trip."

"Thank you!" he replied.

George quietly breathed a sigh of relief. He stuck his passport in his pocket and gently smiled. Those few passengers who were taken off the bus never made it back. They were escorted back to the Canadian side of the border for not having the proper documents to enter the U.S.

About five miles away from the border the bus made a stop at a rest area for people to stretch little. George got off last and found Silvia waiting. They had it arranged that way.

She did not recognize him. He looked like he aged by years from all he had been through. She, on the other hand, did not change much, except a few grey hairs that showed here and there. They both laughed, gave each other a quick hug, and walked towards Silvia's car. As they drove to town George admired everything on the way, including the trees and the air.

He rolled down the window and took a big breath of air, then looking at Silvia saying, "Good to be home! I missed waking up to this every morning. I missed the people especially." His look to Silvia said something that he could not utter aloud, but she could read his heart from his voice.

The Big Apple hadn't changed much. It looked the same as George remembered it. He had spent a long time in it and loved living there. New York City was home for him. Silvia had already arranged a place for him to stay or hide. She rented him an apartment on the outskirts of Brooklyn with an assumed name she dug up from the CIA database. It was an agent killed years ago in a drug deal operation. She had a fake ID made with the name of Jeff Waters from Burbank , CA. "Jeff" had moved to NYC to take a job as a senior loan officer with City Bank at the Rockefeller Center. Nobody ever checked if George was really who he said he was, not even the bank where he opened an account. He was known as "Mr. Waters." Silvia stayed away from the place where George was hiding. She would call couple of times a week to make sure everything was okay.

Two weeks went by after George came back, but nothing suspicious happened. He needed a plan to get his operation in motion. On a Saturday when Silvia called, he picked up the phone.

"Hello," he said.

"Hey, it's me," Silvia replied.

"How is it going?" he asked.

Good! Listen, something came up that I think you should know about."

"What is it?" George asked, curious.

"Scott Canwell is supposedly dead," she said.

"How?" George stood up from his chair, surprised.

"They said he never woke up from his sleep," Silvia explained.

"This is not the case. I am sure something is up and someone is behind it," George said. "Can you get me Skip's phone number? Not his office, better his cell phone."

"Where do I find it?" Silvia asked.

"Just call him and tell him George needs your cell phone number," George explained.

"I'll call his office on Monday," she replied.

"Don't bring up Scott's name when you call him. This is not out yet." Silvia made sure George wouldn't say anything.

"Okay, talk to you Monday then." They both hung up.

Skip was out that week, as he had to travel to Russia to deal with a messy case of two CIA agents framed and jailed by the Russian government for money laundering and drug trafficking. He was meeting with the head of Russian Intelligence to negotiate a deal to bring the two agents home. Silvia spoke to his secretary and was told she should call back on Thursday.

Meanwhile, George decided to venture out to find a cyber café where he could take a look at the contents of the flash drive Rupert gave him. He found a place not too far away, took a chair at the computer station, and plugged in his stick. He typed in the password "Cayman Island," Rupert's favorite place. Rupert never told anyone about his plan to go to the Grand Cayman with the stolen diamonds, which was why he protected the drive with that password until George got it from him.

The computer screen read *Confidential.* It showed a list of names that were not familiar to George. The flash drive had code names and addresses of some secret locations where clandestine meetings were held, George suspected.

He spent couple of hours trying to figure out what to do with the information drive, but it was all unfamiliar to him until he saw Philip's and Scott's names on that list. Under each of the two names was written "Swiss Bank" with what looked like a series of numbers resembling a bank account number.

George ejected the drive, pulled it out, paid the young lady at the counter, and walked out. He now had information that could turn some heads at the Agency. On his way back to the apartment, he stopped at a convenience store where he bought some tape, a pair of scissors, a sewing needle, and thread. At home he flipped the couch over and cut a small opening in the far end of the right leg, where the leg is connected to the fabric.

He wrapped the drive in paper, tying it with a piece of tape, and then sewed the fabric back to the leg of the couch. Even if someone came in looking, they would not look that closely to find the drive, he figured. As for the diamonds, he did not know exactly what to do. He would have given them to Rupert's family, but he did not know if he had one. Rupert had spent most of his life on the streets of Jersey and he never talked to George about a family.

Monday morning, as planned, Silvia called Skip after looking up his direct line on the employee directory.

"Hello," Skip picked up after the second ring.

"Good morning, sir. This is Silvia with the Fusion Center."

"Good morning," Skip replied, waiting for a reason for the call.

"George Munssif asked me to call you and ask for your cell phone number," she explained.

"Where is George?" Skip asked.

"He is in town," Silvia carefully answered, and then quickly stopped the questioning. "I am sure he'll call you soon, once he gets your number," she continued.

"Sure, here it is," and Skip gave her the Manhattan area code number.

"This is your cell, correct?" Silvia insisted.

"Yes! Tell George I'll be waiting to hear from him," Skip commented before hanging up the phone.

The following day George called Skip. Even though the number showed *Unavailable,* Skip knew it was George.

"Hello, this is Skip," he answered.

"George speaking," George said.

"How is it going, George?" Skip asked.

"Fine!" he said with an air of defiance.

"What's up?" Skip asked.

"We need to talk and I'd rather meet than talk by phone," George said.

"Where are you calling from?" Skip knew from Silvia that George was in town, but for some reason he wanted to hear it directly from George.

"From the city," George replied.

"Why don't you come to my office so we can talk?" Skip suggested.

"I prefer if we meet somewhere else," George responded.

"Any place in particular?" Skip asked.

George thought about Skip's question for a minute. "Let's meet at the Times Square subway entrance— 47nd Street and 7th Avenue at 9 a.m."

"See you there," Skip replied.

On Thursday at 8:30 a.m., George was keeping an eye on the subway station entrance to see if Skip or anyone else suspicious showed up. He hid for a while, waiting until it was past 9:00. Then he saw Skip walking into the station alone. He waited until 9:15 before he made his way to the station entrance. Skip was pacing around waiting, when George came from behind him.

"Sorry, I am little late," George apologized.

"Hey, George," Skip replied.

They shook hands. The station was very crowded with people going in different directions.

"Let's take a walk," George suggested. "How much time do you have?" he asked Skip.

"I am okay. My first meeting is not until after lunch," Skip replied.

George headed to the vending machine, inserted few dollars, and bought couple of tickets. Skip did not react to that, except saying, "You did not tell me we going somewhere".

"I can't take any chances." That's all George said.

They boarded the subway. George stood next to the door while Skip leaned against the window.

"What's going on?" Skip was now getting impatient.

"What the hell happened to me during my mission?" George said. "I was chased, kidnapped, jailed, people tried to kill me, and I led a life of a fugitive. What's the story?" George demanded. "And when I asked you to fly me back home, you told me you couldn't. Why?"

"I couldn't just fly you back. You know the protocol. After we talked, I spoke with Philip Lawson and Scott Conwell because they were in charge of the mission, and their thoughts were that you should stay until the mission was complete," Skip explained.

"You spoke to whom?" George asked surprised. "No, this can't be. You're kidding, right?"

"Remember? You know Philip and Scott are in charge of the Africa, the Middle East, and Asia regions. Any feedback on agents deployed to those areas, Philip and Scott are first to consult," Skip continued.

"Tell me again. What do you know about Operation Stone," George kept pressing Skip.

"You already asked this question when you called me from Pakistan," Skip said.

"Yes, I did and can't remember what you told me," George replied.

"Operation Stone was about diamond trafficking in Africa and Europe. Philip and Scott were in charge of that operation, from what I know," Skip commented.

"Did anything happen with Operation Stone? Is it still alive?" George asked.

"No, not anymore. Someone pulled the plug on the operation. No idea why," Skip told George.

"Rupert was killed because of Operation Stone. When he found out that Philip and Scott were involved in the blood diamond business, they sent him to Pakistan and then they decided to kill him."

"These are serious accusations, you realize." Skip was looking straight into George's face.

"I am not just accusing them. I have proof of what I am telling you," George said, surprising Skip.

"What proof?" Skip asked.

"Rupert wasn't just an agent. He was one of them. He worked with them until he decided to steal some diamonds and disappear," George said.

"Philip and Scott were afraid that Rupert was going to spill everything he knew, so they had to kill him," George explained.

"He had a flash drive with some agents' names involved in the operation, Jamil Chehab, Philip, Scott and others," George went on.

"Where is this drive?" Skip asked.

"Somewhere safe," George replied.

"Can I see it?" Skip requested

"At the right time you will," George responded.

George was still not sure if he should trust Skip, but he was willing to play the game for as long as it took to get to Philip.

The subway stopped at the next stop. "This is my stop," George told Skip. "You can keep going or you can get off here," he continued.

Skip decided to stay on and get off two stops later, closer to his work. "Let me know what you want to do," Skip yelled at George.

"I'll be in touch," George replied before disappearing in the crowd.

Upon his arrival home, he phoned Silvia and told her where the drive was hidden if something went wrong. Silvia asked him if he had talked to Skip.

"Yes, I just got back from meeting with him," George said.

"Anything new?" she asked.

"He seems to have no idea what Scott and Philip were doing," George replied.

"Did you tell him about the drive?" she continued.

"Yeah, he wanted to know where it was, but I didn't tell him," George said. "What's the latest about Scott's death?"

"Not much. Some are saying he was having some personal problems, and he might have had a heart attack while sleeping. A memo went out today to all employees to let them know he died," she said.

"I need to get to Philip," George muttered.

"You need to what?" Silvia asked.

"No, nothing, just something I remembered," George replied. He didn't want her to get involved, knowing that Silver Head took anyone who got in his way. "What are you doing tomorrow after work?" he asked

"No plans," Silvia answered.

George wanted to see her, this time not to ask for help. His feelings for her had grown, and so had hers for him. They showed signs of deep affection for each other, but George was afraid of what might come. The situation he was in held him back every time he tried telling her how exactly how he felt towards her. Silvia knew that and didn't push. She knew it would happen when the right time came. For now, she just wanted George to get out of the mess he was in.

They agreed to meet not too far from her work. Café Fato was on their mind, but George suggested another place, because he didn't want to run into anyone who might recognize him.

They decided to meet in a hotel restaurant for dinner. The veal shank George ordered was braised in a reduced wine sauce, garnished with melted Roquefort cheese. It came with a side of small red potatoes arranged in a puzzle shape with strips of mixed melted butter and chives. Silvia, on the other hand, went light. Her favorite dish was sea bass in a lemon sauce, garnished with black olives and capers. Hers came with a side of spinach and garlic mashed potatoes. For dessert they opted for homemade cheesecake and two cappuccinos.

During dinner the discussion started with George meeting Skip, also touching on Philip, Scott and Rupert. George was totally convinced that Scott was eliminated by Philip and tried to give Silvia the reasons why. She was listening attentively to everything George said. He even told her about his dad and what happened to him.

The conversation seemed tightly focused, when suddenly it took a different turn. George decided to open up to Silvia. She wasn't expecting such an event but was quite interested to hear what George was keeping inside for so long. She wrapped her hands around her coffee cup, looked at him straight in the face, and smiled every time he said her name. She could hardly wait for her turn to speak. Although they had been apart for some time and never had an opportunity to reveal their feelings to each other, anybody could tell how close they were.

George went on talking for a while before he stopped, apologizing for talking for so long. Silvia didn't mind that a bit. She was so happy at that moment, more than any other time. George was thrilled that he had finally found the courage to express his true feelings to her and yet, he was afraid of her response. Silvia didn't have to give George any answer, as her heart through her facial expression, had already told George what he was hoping to hear.

The light rain and a late evening breeze around 9:30 gave George a good alibi to accompany Silvia to the subway, and unlike their first meeting at Café Fato when he offered to walk her to her car, this time she did not oppose it. In fact, she welcomed his offer with her arm tucked under his arm, walking slowly and enjoying every moment of their time together. George wanted to take her to her house, but she told him not worry, she would be fine. She even promised to call him once she arrived home. After a few minutes waiting for the train to show up, she hopped on it while George stood there waving goodbye. She waved back from behind the window as the train pulled away from the station.

George's happiness didn't last long. When he got home, he found everything upside down, his furniture, clothes, and everything else he had. He stopped at the doorstep, hesitating to go in. His eyes went straight to the couch. He wanted to rush and check if the drive was still there but stood still in case someone was present.

He grabbed a long necked vase that was sitting close to the door and proceeded slowly towards the center of the living room. He walked quietly to the bedroom, where he saw everything he owned on the floor. Even the light bulbs from his night stand lights were removed and thrown on his bed. He rushed back to the living room, flipped the couch, and was relieved to see that no one noticed the place where he had hidden the drive. He opened the small cut he had made, removed the plastic bag, and stuffed it in his pocket.

He knew whoever was in his apartment would come back. He wondered who did it. His mind went straight to Skip, because he was the only one who knew George was back and that the drive was in New York. George picked up the phone to call Skip but decided to call Silvia instead to make sure she was okay.

The time was late, about 11:30, when Silvia's phone rang. She wasn't asleep, as she was still thinking about everything George had told her.

"Hello!" she said. She knew it was George.

"Hey, are you okay?" George asked.

"Yes, why?" she asked.

"Someone was in my place. It's a mess here, and they've been through everything," he said.

"Did they take anything?" she asked.

"They were probably looking for the drive," George replied, "but they didn't find it."

"Who could it have been?" Silvia asked.

"I don't know," George replied. "The only person who knows I am in town is Skip, and this happened right after I met with him."

"You think Skip is behind it?" Silvia asked.

"I don't know! Nobody else knows about the drive," George replied.

Silvia paused for a minute.

"Are you still there?" George asked.

"Yes, yes, sorry. I was thinking, if it's not Skip, then Philip must be the one," she said.

"Philip doesn't know I am back. Wait, unless Skip told him," George wondered.

"Are you going to ask Skip?" she asked.

"I'll call him tomorrow," George replied.

Silvia was smart. She suggested that George not directly ask Skip. Instead, he should ask Skip if he still spoke with Philip. George liked the idea.

The next day, George got on the phone with Skip.

"Hello, Hallway speaking," Skip answered the phone, for the first time using his last name.

"Hey, Skip. George here," he said.

"Hello George. How are you doing?" Skip replied. "What's going on?"

"Am I still on the Agency's payroll?" George started the conversation

"As far as I know, you are. Why?" Skip answered.

"Just curious to know what happened after you sent me on the mission," George continued. "I recall that Philip was in charge of the Middle East department which I was part of."

"Yes, I remember that. In fact, Philip called me couple of days ago asking what happened to your mission in the Middle East. I told him I'll have to look into it," Skip explained.

Hearing this made George realize that Philip would never give up trying to put his hands on that flash drive.

"What happened since our last discussion?" Skip asked. "Are you going to come forward with the proof you have?"

At the right time I will," George replied. "I had some visitors in my place. They turned the whole apartment upside down looking for something."

"You mean the drive you told me about?" Skip asked.

"I don't know what they were looking for." George dodged the question.

"Any idea who that might be?" Skip asked.

"No," George replied, even though he knew Philip was somehow involved.

"What's your plan now?" Skip asked.

"Don't know." George refused to share any information with Skip. That was the end of the phone call, as George wanted to keep it short so he didn't have to answer too many questions.

George's next move was to go straight after Philip. He didn't want to waste any more time getting to the bottom of the situation. He managed again with the help of Silvia to get Philip's contact information.

"This is Lawson," Philip answered the call.

"I will not leave you alone until you pay for what you did to Rupert," George said with an angry voice.

"Who is speaking?" Philip asked.

"That's not important," George replied. "Understand that eliminating Scott is not going to get you off."

George could not see Philip's face, but he could tell Philip was very uncomfortable from his voice.

"Hello, hello, hello?" Philip repeated, but the phone went dead.

He grabbed his jacket and stormed out to the underground garage of the building, got in his BMW, and left in such a hurry that he almost hit a by passer. George was watching him from a phone booth across the street from the building where he placed the call. However, George didn't know where he was going and couldn't follow him.

Philip rushed to his house, removed a picture frame from the wall, opened the safe, and pulled out a bunch of papers and another small handheld safe. He stuck a key in it, opened it, and pulled a bag stuffed with diamonds and his loaded Glock 33 357SIG subcompact. He threw everything in a brief case and rushed back to his car.

He dialed a number on his cell phone. "This is Philip," he said in a nervous tone. "I just got a call from somebody mentioning Rupert and Scott. I think this whole freaking deal is blown!"

"Nothing is blown. Just be quiet and listen," the voice on the line said.

"You need to get this mess cleaned up before it's too late," Philip commented.

"This is not a phone conversation. Where are you? Let's meet at the usual place," the voice said.

"I'll be there in 15 minutes," Philip replied.

Philip pulled up in his car, got out, locked the briefcase in the trunk, and proceeded toward the door of a house located on the north side of town in a subdivision with an upscale neighborhood. The house belonged to the Agency and was used to temporarily house witnesses who joined the Witness Protection Program but had been vacant for some time.

Philip unlocked the door, walked in, and sat on a chair by the window looking at the street. A few minutes later, he stood up, stuck his fingers between the blinds, and took a look outside. He saw nothing particular; the street was empty except a few cars coming and going. He walked to the kitchen, grabbed a glass of water, took his medication out of his pocket, and swallowed it. He had high blood pressure for which he was taking a prescription.

He heard someone opening the door and walking in. He set the glass down and moved cautiously toward the door, when he saw a shadow of a body standing at the entrance. He couldn't see who it was, though. Philip was very smart and could sense when something was not right. As a trained agent, he could take anything and turn it into a weapon. He removed his tiepin, turned it around so the sharp end protruded, stuck it between his middle fingers, and made his hand into a fist. He waited there for few minutes, ready to strike whoever was standing at the entrance.

The footsteps came closer. Philip positioned himself, ready to deliver the deadly blow. Suddenly, Jamil Chehab stood still in front of Philip. Without saying anything, Philip shook his head.

He lowered his fist and looked at Jamil with an angry glare.

Jamil quickly asked, "What did he say about Rupert and Scott?"

"He said something about eliminating Rupert and Scott?" Philip replied in an uncomfortable way. "He sounded like he knew a lot from his phone call," he continued.

"Did you trace the call?" Jamil asked.

"No, I left right after the call," Philip answered.

"We need to keep a low profile for a while," Jamil suggested. "No phone calls, no meetings until we see what this guy is up to. Get rid of anything you have. No trace, you hear me?" he ordered. "For now, don't do anything. Wait until you hear from me."

Philip waited about 15 minutes after Jamil left before he made his way out. That evening the only place that sounded right was a local bar. He walked in ordered, a drink, and scrolled through his phone, deleting messages both voice and text. He sat at the bar for some time, consuming several drinks until he could barely stand on his feet. The bar tender asked him if he wanted a cab, but he refused. He paid his tab and left.

Philip drove his car outside town where he checked into a small motel. He thought about different scenarios, from being arrested and prosecuted to even killing Jamil Chehab. He opened the briefcase and rummaged through some folders, pictures, and bank accounts. He put them in the bathroom sink and burned them. Then he picked up the remaining ashes and flushed them down the toilet.

Late the next morning, he checked out of the hotel and went to work acting normally, just as Jamil Chehab asked him.

Although he tried to behave his best, his mind was not all there. He sat in his office most of the day, instructing his secretary not to transfer any calls unless it was an emergency and to cancel all his meetings. He felt trapped, desperate for a solution now that he knew serious troubles are not far away in Pakistan or Afghanistan, but very close. While thinking of a plan, his secretary buzzed him.

"Sir, someone is insisting to speak with you."

I said, no phone calls," he angrily replied.

"But this gentleman said that you would talk to him. His name is George," she continued.

Philip was shocked into inaction for a moment. "What's his name again?" He wanted to confirm.

"George Munssif," the secretary said.

"Put him through," Philip ordered.

"Philip here," he said, pretending to sound very normal.

"Did your secretary hand you today's mail?" George asked. "Look through it, there is a little gift for you," he continued in a sarcastic way.

Philip grabbed the mail sitting on his desk and checked it. He found an envelope with no return address and opened it to see a copy of a disk and some photos.

Philip's only response to that was "Can we meet and talk?" He was too familiar with phone tapping. It was his job, and he did not want to take a chance.

"Name the place," George arrogantly replied.

"How about McLeod Tea Room on Main Street?" Philip proposed. "7 p.m."

"You'd better be alone," George warned Philip.

George's plan was now in motion. After hanging up with Philip, he called Silvia first and told her he was meeting with Philip tonight at McLeod Tea Room If she didn't hear from him later that night, she should give the drive and the diamonds to Skip. She knew where they were.

"Sure! Be careful." She finally said it! "I love you!"

"Love you too! Call you later," George replied.

He then called Skip.

"Hey, George. What's up?" Skip asked.

"I am meeting Philip tonight and I need a favor," George said.

"What it is?" Skip asked.

"I need to record the conversation with him. Can you arrange for that?" George asked.

"On such a short notice? I don't know, but let me see what I can do," Skip replied. "Call me back in an hour." Skip knew he could pull it off but wanted to make sure that George was up to it and not just blowing smoke.

An hour later, Skip's phone rang. "Okay, George, where do you want to do this?" he asked.

"I'll come to your office," George announced. I can be there around 6."

"See you then," Skip replied.

At 6 o'clock sharp, George showed up at Skip's office. Skip had the recorder and wire sitting on his desk.

"Where are you meeting him?" Skip asked.

"McLeod Tea Room," George replied without hesitation. However, George didn't give the exact time.

"Do you need me to be there?" Skip asked.

"No, I'll be fine. But I told Silvia if anything goes wrong to hand you the drive and something else," George explained. He did not want to mention the diamonds in case there was a change in the plan.

Skip helped George put on the wire and hide the recorder.

"Let me know once the meeting is over." Skip said.

"Sure thing. Thanks!" George replied on his way out.

At 7: 15 Philip walked in to the tearoom. George was already there but kept at a distance to make sure Philip was alone. A few minutes after Philip sat down, George approached the table, pulled over a chair, and sat facing the door.

"Listen, I'll make this short," Philip started. "You have no idea who you are messing with. The situation is beyond what you can handle. My advice to you is to forget the whole thing, hand me the drive, and move on." Philip was trying his best to intimidate George.

"We can make your life either miserable or give you enough money to live the rest of your life like a king. Your choice," Philip proposed.

"No amount of money can make up for what you and your dogs did," George replied. "There is nothing you or your friends can do. The copy you saw isn't only one. I can have all that information all over the news and Agency by tomorrow. If something happen to me, you will go down so fast that you'll have no idea what hit you." George was now playing the intimidation game.

"You screwed up big time—the blood diamonds, killing Rupert, trying to frame me and get me killed, and then Scott. Who else is on your dirty list?" George pushed for answers.

"This is not a game you can play. Mind your own business and forget the whole thing," Philip said.

"This is my game. You got me involved in it, and I intend to play it until the end," George explained.

In the middle of the heated conversation, George glanced toward the door to see two men walking in looking around. He had a feeling that Philip set him up. He quickly jumped out of the chair and ran toward the back of the room. He passed the bathroom and then fled from the back exit.

Philip waved to the two men to follow him. The three of them ran, making their way between the tables with people watching. Once they went through the back exit, George was long gone. They ran to the end of the street but couldn't find him. Philip was outraged that George slipped from his planned execution.

The proof George was looking for was now in his possession. The recording and the drive were all that was needed to make Philip pay for what he did. George called Silvia, telling her that he got Philip. He also called Skip.

"I have the recording," George told him.

"Are you going to bring it?" Skip asked

"I will, but on one condition," George replied. "You help me get Philip to trial."

"That's not a problem if you have the proof," Skip commented.

A couple of days later, George set up a meeting with Skip to hand him the tape, the drive, and the diamonds. He had already made a few copies, leaving two of them with Silvia and two in a safe deposit box at his bank.

Skip gathered all the information he needed to arrest Philip. He even discussed the case with A.W., the CIA Director, about his plan to arrest Philip. A.W. had no objections. In fact, he gave Skip a full clearance to act, but before that happened, he wanted to meet in person with Philip to hear from him directly what he had to say.

The same week, A.W. called Philip to his office. A.W. was direct and didn't like wasting time.

"What happened to Rupert and Scott? And what happened in Kenya with your Middle Eastern contacts?" he interrogated.

"I have no idea what you're referring to, sir," Philip replied.

A.W. smiled, almost laughing. "You know exactly what I am talking about," he shouted. "I'll ask you once again, who killed Rupert? Who went after George Munssif in Pakistan and Afghanistan? And who killed Scott?

"Because Rupert knew too much and was ready to talk, you killed him. Scott was also killed for the same reason, and George knew everything from Rupert, so you thought he must go too."

Philip did not answer. The only statement he repeated was, "I don't know, sir, what you are talking about."

"Meeting's over." A.W. pointed to the door. As Philip started walking Away, A.W. ordered him, "Leave your badge here. The case is under investigation, and you're off duty until the investigation is over."

Philip took off his badge and set it on A.W.'s desk before leaving.

A.W. rang his secretary. "Find me Skip Hallaway," he ordered her.

"Yes, sir!" she replied.

A few minutes later, Skip was on the phone. "I had Philip in my office. You need to get this case closed as soon as possible before the freaking newspapers get ahold of the story and screw up the Agency."

Meanwhile, as soon as Philip left A.W.'s office, he called Jamil.

"Didn't I tell you not to call me and to keep low for a while?" Jamil yelled on the phone.

"Look, this is getting out of hand! A.W. just called me to his office. He seemed to know the whole story. You need to do something," Philip said, frustrated.

"Did you get rid of the stuff?" Jamil asked.

"Yeah, listen, this thing is going to blow. We can't wait!" Philip yelled.

Jamil asked Philip to end the call, as even his cell phone could be tapped.

A week later Philip was found dead in the same hotel he had checked into a week earlier after leaving the bar. He overdosed himself with his blood pressure medication and Black Label.

A few months later Jamil was arrested by Interpol in a small town in Dubai living under a different identity. He was brought back to the U.S to face charges of murder, conspiracy to commit fraud, racketeering, blood diamond smuggling, and money laundering. He was sentenced to 30 years in jail.

As for George and Silvia, they got married July 5th in Lebanon. Isabella was so happy that day. George and Silvia flew back to the U.S. a couple of weeks after the wedding. They had a small reception at Café Fato, mainly for Silvia's friends.

Mama Alberta was happy to see both George and Silvia together again. She welcomed them with her usual jokes. "I knew from the first time I saw you two that you were meant for each other."

Skip was among the guests. He pulled George aside and gave him the news that Philip apparently took his own life and Jamil was arrested. Skip asked George to come back, and as a wedding gift, he handed him his new badge and business card reading, *George Munssif, Director of Operations.* The fictional company was a medical supply firm based in New York with branches in the Far East. The company's name was U.S. Med Corp.

George looked at the badge and the card, hesitating to accept Skip's gift, but deep down he felt excitement. He accepted the new job. Silvia saw both Skip and George talking. She also saw George holding the card in his hand. She later asked him what Skip was talking to him about. For the first time in their relationship he could not tell her the truth.

"That was Skip's new business card," George said. "Apparently, he has a new job with the Agency," he continued.

The couple continued living in New York City, settling down in their new married life. George took Skip's offer, working with the medical supply company, and Silvia returned to her job with the Fusion Center. For months life was quiet for both of them. They saw each other every day. Some days they met outside their work for coffee or lunch, and in the evenings they were both home.

Their time together was very precious, and they enjoyed every minute of it, until the day Skip called George, asking him to travel to Egypt for a mission. Based on credible sources, the threat involved a plot to kidnap and possibly kill two highly placed State Department officials who were in Egypt for a classified meeting with the new interim government after toppling Mubarak's 40 years old regime...

www.ingramcontent.com/pod-product-compliance
Lightning Source LLC
Chambersburg PA
CBHW070026120726
47909CB00003B/1077